STORIES FROM OVID
A COLLECTION SELECTED AND
TRANSLATED FROM LATIN

HARRY LIUHAN

FIRST PUBLISHED IN 2024

Stories from Ovid
Harry Liuhan
© Harry Liuhan 2024

ISBN: 9798873885633

DEDICATION:

I dedicate this book for my mother and father
Jing and Jun
and my cat
Snowball

INTRODUCTION

This Book contains a collection of Ovid's stories with an English parallel translation opposite the Latin text. The book's intended purpose is to provide Latin enthusiasts with something that they can use to improve their Latin by having a parallel translation which makes learning the structure and grammar of Latin easier whilst having something to refer. Readers can also read the translation for enjoyment purposes and immerse themselves in ancient Roman literature.

I wanted to write this book because I found learning Latin through school and textbooks quite boring and I felt like parallel text is the most efficient and fun way of learning Latin, however I couldn't find many translations relevant to school work, GCSEs and on to A-levels, so I created this book which is a selection of stories relevant to school work but also provides some insight into the tales of Ovid and some fun whilst learning.

This book is a carefully selected collection of stories by Ovid, presented with the original Latin text alongside an English translation. Its purpose is to offer a more engaging and effective way to learn Latin, especially for students preparing for their GCSEs and A-Levels. Traditional methods of learning Latin often rely on textbooks and can be uninteresting. This book aims to change that by providing a side-by-side comparison of Latin and English, making it easier to understand Latin structure and grammar.

The idea for this book came from my own experiences of finding Latin lessons boring and the lack of suitable parallel texts for school coursework. By including stories that are not only relevant to the curriculum but also interesting, this book helps students learn Latin in a more enjoyable way. It offers insight into Ovid's tales, adding an element of fun to the learning process.

In summary, this book is designed to be both a helpful study tool and an enjoyable read, bringing to life the stories of Ovid and making Latin learning more accessible and engaging.

Publius Ovidius Naso, known as Ovid, was a Roman poet born on March 20, 43 BC, in Sulmo (modern Sulmona), Italy. He was a contemporary of Augustus and lived during the early Roman Empire's golden age. Educated in Rome and later in Athens, Ovid initially pursued a career in public service but soon turned to poetry, where his talents flourished.

Ovid's poetic works are diverse, but he is best known for three major works: "Amores" (Love Affairs), "Ars Amatoria" (The Art of Love), and "Metamorphoses." "Metamorphoses," his most renowned work, is an epic narrative poem that weaves together various mythological and historical tales, all connected by the theme of transformation.

His poetry is characterised by its wit, inventive storytelling, and eloquent verse. Ovid's work often explored love, mythological themes, and the interaction between humans and gods. Unlike his contemporaries Virgil and Horace, Ovid's work had a more playful and irreverent tone, which sometimes led to controversy. His "Ars Amatoria," a guide on love and seduction, was possibly one of the reasons cited for his banishment by Emperor Augustus to Tomis (now Constanța, Romania) in 8 AD, where he lived in exile until his death in 17 AD.

Ovid's poetry remains popular for several reasons:

1.   Universal Themes: Ovid's exploration of love, transformation, and the human condition resonates across centuries. His stories capture a range of human emotions and experiences that remain relevant.

2.   Artistic Influence: "Metamorphoses" has been a significant influence on Western art and literature. Its stories have inspired countless works, from Shakespeare's plays to modern novels and films.

3.   Literary Merit: Ovid was a master of the Latin language, and his skilful use of meter, narrative structure, and poetic devices make his work a high point of Latin literature.

4.   Cultural Insight: His works provide valuable insights into Roman culture, mythology, and society, offering a window into the ancient world.

5.   Accessibility: Ovid's style is more accessible than some of his contemporaries, with a clear, engaging narrative style that appeals to a broad audience.

In summary, Ovid's enduring popularity stems from his ability to blend artistic mastery with universally resonant themes, making his work a timeless exploration of human nature and experience.

THE FAME OF ARION
OVID'S FASTI II
LINES 79–118

1 Quem modo caelatum stellis Delphina videbas,
is fugiet visus nocte sequente tuos,
seu fuit occultis felix in amoribus index,
Lesbida cum domino seu tulit ille lyram.
2 quod mare non novit, quae nescit Ariona tellus?
carmine currentes ille tenebat aquas.
3 saepe sequens agnam lupus est a voce retentus,
saepe avidum fugiens restitit agna lupum;
saepe canes leporesque umbra iacuere sub una,
et stetit in saxo proxima cerva leae,
et sine lite loquax cum Palladis alite cornix sedit,
et accipitri iuncta columba fuit.
4 Cynthia saepe tuis fertur, vocalis Arion,
tamquam fraternis obstipuisse modis.
5 nomen Arionium Siculas impleverat urbes
captaque erat lyricis Ausonis ora sonis;
inde domum repetens puppem conscendit Arion,
atque ita quaesitas arte ferebat opes.
6 forsitan, infelix, ventos undasque timebas:
at tibi nave tua tutius aequor erat.
7 namque gubernator destricto constitit ense
ceteraque armata conscia turba manu.
8 quid tibi cum gladio? dubiam rege, navita, puppem:
non haec sunt digitis arma tenenda tuis.
9 ille, metu pavidus, 'mortem non deprecor' inquit,
'sed liceat sumpta pauca referre lyra.'
10 dant veniam ridentque moram: capit ille coronam,
quae possit crines, Phoebe, decere tuos;
induerat Tyrio bis tinctam murice pallam:
reddidit icta suos pollice chorda sonos,
flebilibus numeris veluti canentia dura
traiectus penna tempora cantat olor.
11 protinus in medias ornatus desilit undas;
spargitur impulsa caerula puppis aqua.
12 inde (fide maius) tergo delphina recurvo
se memorant oneri subposuisse novo.
13 ille, sedens citharamque tenens, pretiumque vehendi
cantat et aequoreas carmine mulcet aquas.
14 di pia facta vident: astris delphina recepit
Iuppiter et stellas iussit habere novem.

1 Whom you recently saw as a dolphin marked by the stars,
will escape your eyes the following night,
either he was a fortunate indicator in concealed love affairs,
or he carried with his master the Lesbian lyre.
2 What land does not know, Arion what sea does not know?
His song that held the flowing waters.
3 Often, the wolf following the lamb held by his voice,
often the fleeing lamb restrained the hungry wolf;
often dogs and hares lay under one shadow,
and a deer stood on rocks near a lioness,
and the cawing crows sat with the Palladian owls
without quarrel, the dove joined the hawk.
4 Cynthia is said often to have been moved by your voice,
Arion, as if of her brother Apollo.
5 Arion's name had filled the cities of Sicily and the Italian seashores
were captured by the sound of his lyre;
then Arion returning home boarded a ship,
carrying his wealth acquired through his art.
6 Perhaps, unfortunate, you feared the wind and waves:
but the calm seas was safer for you than your ship.
7 For the steersman stood with blade unsheathed,
and the rest of the crowd was aware of this and armed, hands ready.
8 What needs do you have for your sword? Steer the moving ship:
These weapons are not for your fingers to hold.
9 Arion trembling with fear said 'I don't beg for my life
but allow me to take back my lyre for a bit.'
10 They gave him mercy and laughed at the delay: he took his crown,
which might adorn your hair; Phoebus,
he had put his robe twice dyed in Tyrian purple:
the strings, plucked by his thumb, returned their chorus,
he sang a melody, as a swan is said to sing in its final moments,
pierced by an arrow through its neck.
11 Immediately he plunged into the middle of the waves fully clothed;
the water was scattered by his impact onto the sky blue stern.
12 Then (beyond faith) it is said a dolphin
offered itself to carry the new burden on its curved back.
13 He, sitting and holding his lyre, in singing he paid his fare,
and soothing the sea waters with his song.
14 the gods see good deeds: Jupiter took the dolphin into the galaxy,
and ordered it to have nine stars.

ROMULUS AND REMUS
OVID'S FASTI IV
LINES 809–858

1 iam luerat poenas frater Numitoris, et omne
pastorum gemino sub duce volgus erat;
contrahere agrestes et moenia ponere utrique
convenit: ambigitur moenia ponat uter.
2 'nil opus est' dixit 'certamine' Romulus 'ullo;
magna fides avium est: experiamur aves.'
3 res placet: alter init nemorosi saxa Palati;
alter Aventinum mane cacumen init.
4 sex Remus, hic volucres bis sex videt ordine; pacto
statur, et arbitrium Romulus urbis habet.
5 apta dies legitur qua moenia signet aratro:
sacra Palis suberant; inde movetur opus.
6 fossa fit ad solidum, fruges iaciuntur in ima
et de vicino terra petita solo;
fossa repletur humo, plenaeque imponitur ara,
et novus accenso fungitur igne focus.
7 inde premens stivam designat moenia sulco;
alba iugum niveo cum bove vacca tulit.
8 vox fuit haec regis: 'condenti, Iuppiter, urbem,
et genitor Mavors Vestaque mater, ades,
quosque pium est adhibere deos, advertite cuncti:
auspicibus vobis hoc mihi surgat opus.
9 longa sit huic aetas dominaeque potentia terrae,
sitque sub hac oriens occiduusque dies.'
10 ille precabatur, tonitru dedit omina laevo
Iuppiter, et laevo fulmina missa polo.
11 augurio laeti iaciunt fundamina cives,
et novus exiguo tempore murus erat.
12 hoc Celer urget opus, quem Romulus ipse vocarat,
'sint' que, 'Celer, curae' dixerat 'ista tuae,
neve quis aut muros aut factam vomere fossam
transeat; audentem talia dede neci.'
13 quod Remus ignorans humiles contemnere muros
coepit, et 'his populus' dicere 'tutus erit?'
nec mora, transiluit: rutro Celer occupat ausum;
ille premit duram sanguinulentus humum.
14 haec ubi rex didicit, lacrimas introrsus obortas
devorat et clausum pectore volnus habet.
15 flere palam non volt exemplaque fortia servat,
'sic' que 'meos muros transeat hostis' ait.

1 Now after the brother of Numitor had suffered punishments
and all the gathering of shepherds were under the lead of the twins;
the twins agreed to gather beasts of burden and put up walls and a city:
the question was who should give name to the city;
Romulus said "there is no need for a contest,
since there is great faith in birds, let the birds decide."
2 The matter was settled: one of them entered the rocks of wooded
Palatine; the other to the top of Aventine in the morning.
3 Remus saw six, Romulus saw twice six; with both standing their pacts
Romulus was now the master of the city.
4 A suitable day was chosen for Romulus to mark out the walls with a
plough: the festival of Pales was nearby; hence the work was started
then.
5 they trenched down to solid rocks, threw fruits of harvest,
and at the bottom soil from the ground nearby;
the ditch was filled with soil, and completed with an altar,
and a fire was kindled on the new hearth.
6 Then pressing down the handle of the plough he marked out the
walls; a white cow and snow-white ox bore the yoke.
7 These were the words of the king: 'form with me my city, Jupiter,
father Mars, mother Vesta, and all you gods whom piety summons take
notice: my city will rise with your guiding voices.
8 May it live long and rule over conquered worlds,
and may all from the east to the west be subject to my city.'
9 So he prayed, Jupiter gave him an omen with thunder on his left,
and sent a lightning leftward through the sky.
10 Delighted by the omens the citizens laid the foundations,
and new walls were raised in a short time.
11 the work was urged on by Celer, who was named by Romulus
himself, he said 'Celer be it your care that no one cross the walls nor the
trenches and kill anyone who dares to crosses.'
12 Remus unknowingly began to disparage the small wall,
and to say 'will our city be safe within these walls?'
Without delay, he crossed them: Celer struck the bold man with a
shovel; bloodied Remus fell to the rough ground.
13 When the king learned about this, he suppressed his rising tears
and locked away his grief in his heart.
14 He did not wish to weep in public but maintained an example of
fortitude.
15 He said 'So may all who cross my walls perish.'

16 dat tamen exsequias; nec iam suspendere fletum
sustinet, et pietas dissimulata patet;
osculaque adplicuit posito suprema feretro,
atque ait 'invito frater adempte, vale',
arsurosque artus unxit: fecere, quod ille,
Faustulus et maestas Acca soluta comas.
17 tum iuvenem nondum facti flevere Quirites;
ultima plorato subdita flamma rogo est.
18 urbs oritur (quis tunc hoc ulli credere posset?)
victorem terris impositura pedem.

16 However, he gave funeral processions; and now he couldn't hold his
tears, and the love he his hiding was obvious;
and when they set him down on the last bier, he gave one last kiss
and said 'farewell, brother taken from me',
and he anointed the limbs about to be burned:
Faustulus and Acca unbound their hair in mourning as he did.
17 Then the elders, not yet known as senators, wept for the young man;
and the last pyre, wet with their tears, was set aflame.
18 A city rose that would one day spread its dominion over all the -
though who would have believed that then?

DAEDALUS AND ICARUS
OVID'S METAMORPHOSES VIII
183–235

1 Daedalus interea Creten longumque perosus
exilium tactusque loci natalis amore
clausus erat pelago. **2** 'terras licet' inquit 'et undas
obstruat: et caelum certe patet; ibimus illac:
omnia possideat, non possidet aera Minos.'
3 dixit et ignotas animum dimittit in artes
naturamque novat. **4** nam ponit in ordine pennas
a minima coeptas, longam breviore sequenti,
ut clivo crevisse putes: sic rustica quondam
fistula disparibus paulatim surgit avenis;
tum lino medias et ceris alligat imas
atque ita conpositas parvo curvamine flectit,
ut veras imitetur aves. **5** puer Icarus una
stabat et, ignarus sua se tractare pericla,
ore renidenti modo, quas vaga moverat aura,
captabat plumas, flavam modo pollice ceram
mollibat lusuque suo mirabile patris
impediebat opus. **6** postquam manus ultima coepto
inposita est, geminas opifex libravit in alas
ipse suum corpus motaque pependit in aura;
instruit et natum 'medio' que 'ut limite curras,
Icare,' ait 'moneo, ne, si demissior ibis,
unda gravet pennas, si celsior, ignis adurat:
inter utrumque vola. **7** nec te spectare Booten
aut Helicen iubeo strictumque Orionis ensem:
me duce carpe viam!' pariter praecepta volandi
tradit et ignotas umeris accommodat alas.
8 inter opus monitusque genae maduere seniles,
et patriae tremuere manus; dedit oscula nato
non iterum repetenda suo pennisque levatus
ante volat comitique timet, velut ales, ab alto
quae teneram prolem produxit in aera nido,
hortaturque sequi damnosasque erudit artes
et movet ipse suas et nati respicit alas.
9 hos aliquis tremula dum captat harundine pisces,
aut pastor baculo stivave innixus arator
vidit et obstipuit, quique aethera carpere possent,
credidit esse deos.

1 Meanwhile Daedalus despising Crete and his long exile
filled with love for his homeland he had been shut off by the waves.
2 Daedalus said, "Minos may obstruct our escape by land and sea:
but the sky is certainly available; we will go that way:
Minos rules everything but not the heavens."
3 Saying this he sent his mind away to make new skills unknown and
nature undiscovered.
4 For he begins by placing the smallest feathers in order,
followed by a long and a short, so you might think they grew like a
slope: like how rustic pipes and wild straws rises gradually and unevenly;
then he bound them together with a line in the middle and wax as the
base and having ordered them he bent them into a small curve,
in order to imitate a real wings.
5 The boy, Icarus, stood with him and, not realising that
he was handling what would bring his death,
his mouth only beaming, disturbed the wandering air,
he was catching feathers, softening golden beeswax with his thumb
and his playfulness hindered his father's miraculous work.
6 However, having imposed the ultimate touch on what he began,
the inventor balanced the two wings, with his body in between,
hovered in the moving air;
he ordered his son 'I warn you Icarus, take the middle path,
if you go too low, the waves might burden your wings,
if you go too high, the sun scorches:
go between the two.
7 And I order you not to watch Boötes or Ursa Major (Helices)
or be drawn to the sword of Orion: take the way I lead!"
Likewise, he gave a lesson of the rules of flight,
fitted the wings on the boy's shoulder.
8 Meanwhile he did work and warned the dangers of flight
the eye sockets of the old man became wet,
the hand of the father trembled;
he gave kisses that was never again repeated to his son,
lifting up his wings flying ahead fearing for his companions,
just like a bird, leads their youthful offspring from high nests into the
air, he encouraged the boy to follow him and taught him the dangerous
art, and he himself moves his wings and he looks back at the wings of
his son.
9 Someone who caught fish with quivering rods,
a shepherd leaning on his cane,
an astonished ploughman who saw them that someone might be able
split the heavens, he believed them to be gods.

10 et iam Iunonia laeva
parte Samos (fuerant Delosque Parosque relictae)
dextra Lebinthos erat fecundaque melle Calymne,
cum puer audaci coepit gaudere volatu
deseruitque ducem caelique cupidine tractus
altius egit iter. **11** rapidi vicinia solis
mollit odoratas, pennarum vincula, ceras;
tabuerant cerae: nudos quatit ille lacertos,
remigioque carens non ullas percipit auras,
oraque caerulea patrium clamantia nomen
excipiuntur aqua, quae nomen traxit ab illo.
12 at pater infelix, nec iam pater, 'Icare,' dixit,
'Icare,' dixit 'ubi es? qua te regione requiram?'
'Icare' dicebat: pennas aspexit in undis
devovitque suas artes corpusque sepulcro
condidit, et tellus a nomine dicta sepulti.

10 Now on the left was Samos Juno's sacred lands (Delos and Paros were behind),

on the right was Lebinthos and Calymne which was bathed in honey,

when the boy began to enjoy to fly boldly and deserted his leader,

drawn by his desire for the sky, he flew higher.

11 His vicinity to the scorching sun softened the fragrant wax which bound the wings;

the wax had dissolved: he flapped with bare arms,

without his rowing wings he could not glide any air,

his mouth calling his father's name as he vanished into the dark sea,

which now holds his name.

12 But the unlucky father, now no longer a father said,

"Icarus, Icarus, where are you? To which region should I look for you?

Icarus he was calling: he saw wings in the waves,

cursed his art and buried the body in a tomb,

the land is now called by the name of the buried.

MIDAS
OVID'S METAMORPHOSIS XI
LINES 85–193

1 Nec satis hoc Baccho est, ipsos quoque deserit agros
cumque choro meliore sui vineta Timoli
Pactolonque petit, quamvis non aureus illo
tempore nec caris erat invidiosus harenis.
2 hunc adsueta cohors, satyri bacchaeque, frequentant,
at Silenus abest: titubantem annisque meroque
ruricolae cepere Phryges vinctumque coronis
ad regem duxere Midan, cui Thracius Orpheus
orgia tradiderat cum Cecropio Eumolpo.
3 qui simul agnovit socium comitemque sacrorum,
hospitis adventu festum genialiter egit
per bis quinque dies et iunctas ordine noctes,
et iam stellarum sublime coegerat agmen
Lucifer undecimus, Lydos cum laetus in agros
rex venit et iuveni Silenum reddit alumno.

4 Huic deus optandi gratum, sed inutile, fecit
muneris arbitrium gaudens altore recepto.
5 ille male usurus donis ait 'effice, quicquid
corpore contigero, fulvum vertatur in aurum.'
6 adnuit optatis nocituraque munera solvit
Liber et indoluit, quod non meliora petisset.
7 laetus abit gaudetque malo Berecyntius heros
pollicitique fidem tangendo singula temptat
vixque sibi credens, non alta fronde virentem
ilice detraxit virgam: virga aurea facta est;
tollit humo saxum: saxum quoque palluit auro;
contigit et glaebam: contactu glaeba potenti
massa fit; arentis Cereris decerpsit aristas:
aurea messis erat; demptum tenet arbore pomum:
Hesperidas donasse putes; si postibus altis
admovit digitos, postes radiare videntur;
ille etiam liquidis palmas ubi laverat undis,
unda fluens palmis Danaen eludere posset;
vix spes ipse suas animo capit aurea fingens
omnia. **8** gaudenti mensas posuere ministri
exstructas dapibus nec tostae frugis egentes:
tum vero, sive ille sua Cerealia dextra
munera contigerat, Cerealia dona rigebant,
sive dapes avido convellere dente parabat,

1 Neither did this satisfy Bacchus, and he left the fields themselves
and with a better chorus he sought the vineyard of Mount Tmolus
and Pactolus River, which was not made of gold at that time
nor was envied for its precious sands.
2 His usual cohorts, satyrs and bacchantes, frequented him
but Silenus was absent: the Phrygian farmers had captured him
staggering with age and wine and tied him up with garlands
and led him to king Midas, to whom along with Athenian Eumolpus
Orpheus of Thrace had taught the Bacchus rituals.
3 When the king at once recognised him as a friend and companion of
his worship, he celebrated the arrival of his guest jovially
for ten days and ten nights without stop,
and now on the eleventh day Lucifer had sent off the parade of stars,
when the king joyfully came into
the Lydian fields and returned Silenus to his young foster-child.

4 The god rejoicing at his foster-father's return
he gave Midas the pleasing choice of a gift, but however useless,
since Midas was about to make a bad use of the gift,
He said, "make it that whatever I touch with my body,
will be turned into yellow gold."
5 Bacchus granted his wish and released the harmful gift free
and grieved, that he didn't ask for better.
6 Midas departed happily and rejoicing in his misfortunes
he tries out the gift by touching everything.
7 And he, hardly believing it, no sooner broke of the twig from a tree
than it was made into gold
when he snaps a green trig of a tree it turns into gold
when he picks up a rock from the ground it too became pale gold;
and he touched a clod: and by the power of the touch the clod became a
gold nugget; he gathered the withering harvest: it was a golden harvest;
he held the apple which he picked from a tree:
you might think that the daughter of Hesperus, Hesperides, had given it;
if he moved his fingers to the high doorpost,
the doorpost would have been seen to shine;
even when he had washed his hands in liquid waters,
the water flowing over his hand might have been able to deceive Danae;
his mind barely captured the expectation of forming everything into
gold.
8 While rejoicing, his servants set the tables,
piled it up with a feast neither lacking bread:
then in truth, whether he touched the gift of Ceres with his right hand,
the gift hardened, or banquet was provided with hungry teeth,

lammina fulva dapes admoto dente premebat;
miscuerat puris auctorem muneris undis:
fusile per rictus aurum fluitare videres.

9 Attonitus novitate mali divesque miserque
effugere optat opes et quae modo voverat, odit.
10 copia nulla famem relevat; sitis arida guttur
urit, et inviso meritus torquetur ab auro
ad caelumque manus et splendida bracchia tollens
'da veniam, Lenaee pater! peccavimus' inquit,
'sed miserere, precor, speciosoque eripe damno!'
mite deum numen: Bacchus peccasse fatentem
restituit pactique fide data munera solvit
'ne' ve 'male optato maneas circumlitus auro,
vade' ait 'ad magnis vicinum Sardibus amnem
perque iugum nitens labentibus obvius undis
carpe viam, donec venias ad fluminis ortus,
spumigeroque tuum fonti, qua plurimus exit,
subde caput corpusque simul, simul elue crimen.'
11 rex iussae succedit aquae: vis aurea tinxit
flumen et humano de corpore cessit in amnem;
nunc quoque iam veteris percepto semine venae
arva rigent auro madidis pallentia glaebis.

12 Ille perosus opes silvas et rura colebat
Panaque montanis habitantem semper in antris,
pingue sed ingenium mansit, nocituraque, ut ante,
rursus erant domino stultae praecordia mentis.
13 nam freta prospiciens late riget arduus alto
Tmolus in ascensu clivoque extensus utroque
Sardibus hinc, illinc parvis finitur Hypaepis.
14 Pan ibi dum teneris iactat sua sibila nymphis
et leve cerata modulatur harundine carmen
ausus Apollineos prae se contemnere cantus,
iudice sub Tmolo certamen venit ad inpar.

15 Monte suo senior iudex consedit et aures
liberat arboribus: quercu coma caerula tantum
cingitur, et pendent circum cava tempora glandes.
16 isque deum pecoris spectans 'in iudice' dixit
'nulla mora est.' 17 calamis agrestibus insonat ille
barbaricoque Midan (aderat nam forte canenti)
carmine delenit; post hunc sacer ora retorsit
Tmolus ad os Phoebi: vultum sua silva secuta est.

if he tried with eager bites to tear the food, a thin layer of yellow
covered the food where his teeth touch, if he mixed water with wine,
the other gift of his benefactor, you could see molten gold trickling
through his teeth.

9 Thunderstruck by this strange misfortune,
wealthy but miserable, he tries to flee his wealth, and what he had
wanted moments ago, he now hates.

10 Abundance couldn't help his hunger;
his dry throat burned with thirst, and deservingly he was tormented by
the hated gold, with his hands to the sky and raising his noble arms,
he said, 'forgiveness me, Father Bacchus! I have sinned but pity me,
I beg, and save me from this splendid punishment!"
the will of the gods is pleasant:
Bacchus restored Midas who admitted his sin,
took back the promise that was given
"so you don't stay covered in you gold you foolishly wished for,
go to the great river by Sardis,
make your way up the shining ridge through flowing waters,
until you come to source of the river,
plunge your head and body at the same time into the foaming waters
where it exits the mountains, at once your curse will wash out."

11 The king ascended to the water he was ordered to: his golden force
tinted the river, flowing past his body in the stream;
Even now the seeding fields watered by this ancient vein is drenched in
pale lump of gold.

12 Hating his wealth Midas was living in the woods and countryside,
in mountain caves where Pan always lives, however his dull intelligence
remained, the foolish mind of the master was about to harm himself
again, just like before.

13 The steep and tall Mt. Tmolus at its heights commanded a wide view
of the ocean, it extended from Sardis to small Hypaepae.

14 When Pan was there, he boasted his musical skills to the gentle
nymphs, while regulating the reeds with fixed together with wax,
he dared to despise the song of Apollo against his own,
and entered an unfair contest with Tmolus as the judge.

15 The old judge sat on his mountain and freed his ears of the trees:
only oak leaves encircled his azure hair, and acorns hung around his
hollow temples.

16 Looking at the god of animals said, "nothing will stop my
judgement."

17 he sounded the wild reeds and soothed Midas (who by chance was
near to the music) with a foreign song;
after this holy Tmolus turned his face towards Apollo's face:
his forest followed his face.

18 ille caput flavum lauro Parnaside vinctus
verrit humum Tyrio saturata murice palla
instructamque fidem gemmis et dentibus Indis
sustinet a laeva, tenuit manus altera plectrum;
artificis status ipse fuit. **19** tum stamina docto
pollice sollicitat, quorum dulcedine captus
Pana iubet Tmolus citharae submittere cannas.

20 Iudicium sanctique placet sententia montis
omnibus, arguitur tamen atque iniusta vocatur
unius sermone Midae; nec Delius aures
humanam stolidas patitur retinere figuram,
sed trahit in spatium villisque albentibus inplet
instabilesque imas facit et dat posse moveri:
cetera sunt hominis, partem damnatur in unam
induiturque aures lente gradientis aselli.
21 ille quidem celare cupit turpique pudore
tempora purpureis temptat relevare tiaris;
sed solitus longos ferro resecare capillos
viderat hoc famulus, qui cum nec prodere visum
dedecus auderet, cupiens efferre sub auras,
nec posset reticere tamen, secedit humumque
effodit et, domini quales adspexerit aures,
voce refert parva terraeque inmurmurat haustae
indiciumque suae vocis tellure regesta
obruit et scrobibus tacitus discedit opertis.
22 creber harundinibus tremulis ibi surgere lucus
coepit et, ut primum pleno maturuit anno,
prodidit agricolam: leni nam motus ab austro
obruta verba refert dominique coarguit aures.

18 Apollo's golden hair was surrounded by Parnassian laurels,
his robe dyed in Tyrian purple brushed the earth,
in his left hand held his lyre of gem and Indian ivory,
in his other hand he held a plectrum; he was standing in the position of
a singer.
19 Then plucked the threads so skilfully with his thumb,
which capture Tmolus with its sweetness,
he ordered Pan to submit his reedpipes to the lyre.

20 And the sacred judgement of the old mountain god satisfied
everyone, however the judgement of Midas alone denounced it and
called it unjust; neither did Apollo endure to keep such foolish ears in
human form, but he extended them and covered them up with white
hairs, made them floppy at the base and gave them the ability to move:
though everything else was human, he was sentenced in a single part,
he wore ears of a slow walking donkey.
21 He wanted to hide them and attempted to alleviate the sense of
ugliness by wearing a purple turban;
but a servant who usually cut his long hair with an iron blade saw this,
he did not dare to proclaim the disgrace he had seen,
but wanting to tell it under the world, and unable to keep quiet,
he dug a hole in the ground and whispered to it what kind of ear he saw
of his master, in a tiny voice he spoke to the earth,
buried all he had said under the hole so that everything would be silent
when he had left.
22 However, a thick grove of quivering reeds began to grow, by the
twelfth month when it had matured,
it betrayed its planter: moved by a gentle wind,
it repeated all the words buried by the servant,
told from the earth the secret of Midas' ears.

ORPHEUS AND EURYDICE OVID'S METAMORPHOSIS X 1-85

1 Inde per inmensum croceo velatus amictu
aethera digreditur Ciconumque Hymenaeus ad oras
tendit et Orphea nequiquam voce vocatur.
2 adfuit ille quidem, sed nec sollemnia verba
nec laetos vultus nec felix attulit omen.
3 fax quoque, quam tenuit, lacrimoso stridula fumo
usque fuit nullosque invenit motibus ignes.
4 exitus auspicio gravior: nam nupta per herbas
dum nova Naiadum turba comitata vagatur,
occidit in talum serpentis dente recepto.
5 quam satis ad superas postquam Rhodopeius auras
deflevit vates, ne non temptaret et umbras,
ad Styga Taenaria est ausus descendere porta
perque leves populos simulacraque functa sepulcro
Persephonen adiit inamoenaque regna tenentem
umbrarum dominum pulsisque ad carmina nervis
sic ait: 'o positi sub terra numina mundi,
in quem reccidimus, quicquid mortale creamur,
si licet et falsi positis ambagibus oris
vera loqui sinitis, non huc, ut opaca viderem
Tartara, descendi, nec uti villosa colubris
terna Medusaei vincirem guttura monstri:
causa viae est coniunx, in quam calcata venenum
vipera diffudit crescentesque abstulit annos.
6 posse pati volui nec me temptasse negabo:
vicit Amor. **7** supera deus hic bene notus in ora est;
an sit et hic, dubito: sed et hic tamen auguror esse,
famaque si veteris non est mentita rapinae,
vos quoque iunxit Amor. **8** per ego haec loca plena timoris,
per Chaos hoc ingens vastique silentia regni,
Eurydices, oro, properata retexite fata.
9 omnia debemur vobis, paulumque morati
serius aut citius sedem properamus ad unam.
10 tendimus huc omnes, haec est domus ultima, vosque
humani generis longissima regna tenetis.
11 haec quoque, cum iustos matura peregerit annos,
iuris erit vestri: pro munere poscimus usum;
quodsi fata negant veniam pro coniuge, certum est
nolle redire mihi: leto gaudete duorum.'

1 Veiled in saffron robes, travelling through the immeasurable earth, Hymen went to the Ciconian coast, called by the voice of Orpheus in vain.

2 In fact, he was present (at Orpheus and Eurydice's wedding), but he brought neither established words nor happy looks nor good omens.

3 Not only the touch, which he held, continuously made tear screeching smoke and the fire found no movement.

4 The result was worse than an omen: for while the bride was strolling through grass accompanied by a crown of young Naiads, she was killed having been bitten on the ankle by a viper.

5 Afterwards when the bard of Rhodepe mourned her in the upper world, so that he might attempt to go to the underworld,
he dared to descend through the Styx to gates of Taenaria and he went through the weightless ghosts and those who had received proper burials, he arrive at Persephone and to her husband Pluto,
the one holding the joyless kingdom of shadows
and the strings of his lyre being struck to his song,
he sang thus: 'oh gods of the underworld, to which all, who are created mortal, if I may and it is lawful for me to speak the truth,
I descended here, not to see dark Tartarus, nor to conquer the monster of Medusa with his three necks and snakes: the cause of my journey is my wife, who trampled on a viper which poured venom into her and took away her coming years.

6 If able I would suffer, and I do not deny trying: however, love won.

7 he is a god well known in the world above; whether he is known here I do not know: however I predict him to be her as well,
and if old story of that rape is not a lie, Amor also unites you.

8 I through this place filled with fear, through this vast Chaos and silent desolate realm, Eurydice, I beg you unravel her hastened fate.

9 we are all bound to be yours, and though a little delay is serious but eventually we will rush to your abode.

10 All travel to here, this is the ultimate home,
and you hold the longest rain over the human race.

11 She also is yours, when she live out her right to old age,
she will be a subject of you: so we beg a gift of her possession;
but if fate refuses this indulgence for my wife,
I will not return: you can rejoice in our deaths.'

12 Talia dicentem nervosque ad verba moventem
exsangues flebant animae; nec Tantalus undam
captavit refugam, stupuitque Ixionis orbis,
nec carpsere iecur volucres, urnisque vacarunt
Belides, inque tuo sedisti, Sisyphe, saxo.
13 tunc primum lacrimis victarum carmine fama est
Eumenidum maduisse genas, nec regia coniunx
sustinet oranti nec, qui regit ima, negare,
Eurydicenque vocant: umbras erat illa recentes
14 inter et incessit passu de vulnere tardo.
hanc simul et legem Rhodopeius accipit heros,
ne flectat retro sua lumina, donec Avernas
exierit valles; aut inrita dona futura.
15 carpitur adclivis per muta silentia trames,
arduus, obscurus, caligine densus opaca,
nec procul afuerunt telluris margine summae:
hic, ne deficeret, metuens avidusque videndi
flexit amans oculos, et protinus illa relapsa est,
bracchiaque intendens prendique et prendere certans
nil nisi cedentes infelix arripit auras.
16 iamque iterum moriens non est de coniuge quicquam
questa suo (quid enim nisi se quereretur amatam?)
supremumque 'vale,' quod iam vix auribus ille
acciperet, dixit revolutaque rursus eodem est.

17 Non aliter stupuit gemina nece coniugis Orpheus,
quam tria qui timidus, medio portante catenas,
colla canis vidit, quem non pavor ante reliquit,
quam natura prior saxo per corpus oborto,
quique in se crimen traxit voluitque videri
Olenos esse nocens, tuque, o confisa figurae,
infelix Lethaea, tuae, iunctissima quondam
pectora, nunc lapides, quos umida sustinet Ide.
18 orantem frustraque iterum transire volentem
portitor arcuerat: septem tamen ille diebus
squalidus in ripa Cereris sine munere sedit;
cura dolorque animi lacrimaeque alimenta fuere.
19 esse deos Erebi crudeles questus, in altam
se recipit Rhodopen pulsumque aquilonibus Haemum.

20 Tertius aequoreis inclusum Piscibus annum
finierat Titan, omnemque refugerat Orpheus
femineam Venerem, seu quod male cesserat illi,
sive fidem dederat; multas tamen ardor habebat
iungere se vati, multae doluere repulsae.

12 Orpheus sang so well that the bloodless spirits wept to the chords and movements of the words; Tantalus did not capture the vanishing wave, and Ixion's wheel stopped, the vultures did not pluck his liver, and the Belides parted their water jars, and you, Sisyphus, held firm onto your rock.

13 Then the rumors say that for the first time the faces of the Furies were wet with tears, conquered by his song, and the king and queen could not deny his request, and they called for Eurydice: she was among the recently deceased and her wound made her steps slow.

14 The hero of Rhodope received her, and at the same time not turn his eyes behind him, until he exists the valleys of Avernus; or the gift would be useless.

15 They took the upward path through the silent, steep, and shadowy, riverbed, shadowed with dense fog, going closer to the border of the upper world: he, full of excitement, fearing she was not there turned his eyes to his lover, and immediately she was sent back, and stretching out his arms and grabbed and failing to grab anything, the unlucky man grabbed nothing but the departing air.

16 And now dying again the wife could not complain about her husband – for what was there to complain, his love? – and she called out one last 'farewell', which his ears now scarcely receive, and she turn back into the underworld.

17 Orpheus stunned by the double death of his wife, was afraid like someone who saw the three-headed dog, whose middle neck was chained, not before he stopped trembling, whose nature turned his body into stone, or like Olenos who wished to be charged with your crime unfortunate Lethaea, too arrogant of your beauty, once united hearts, now stone, who guard the moist Mt. Ida.

18 Pleading in vain and wanting to cross (the Styx) again Orpheus was stopped by the ferryman: however for seven days he sat on the bank of the river without nourishment (Ceres is the god of agriculture) and self; pain, resentment and tears were his food.

19 complaining the gods of Erebus to be cruel, he took himself to tall Mt. Rhodope, and windy Mt. Haemus.

20 Three times the sun had ended the year through watery Pisces, and Orpheus fled from all love (Venus is god of love) of women, either because things went badly for him, or he swore faith to him wife; however many had an eagerness to unite with the poet, and many hurt by his rejection.

21 ille etiam Thracum populis fuit auctor amorem
in teneros transferre mares citraque iuventam
aetatis breve ver et primos carpere flores.

21 By all means he was the first of Thracians to transfer his love to young boys and their brief springtime, and first flowering, this other side of manhood.

ECHO AND NARCISSUS
OVID'S METAMORPHOSES III
LINES 339–510

1 Ille per Aonias fama celeberrimus urbes
inreprehensa dabat populo responsa petenti;
prima fide vocisque ratae temptamina sumpsit
caerula Liriope, quam quondam flumine curvo
inplicuit clausaeque suis Cephisos in undis
vim tulit: enixa est utero pulcherrima pleno
infantem nymphe, iam tunc qui posset amari,
Narcissumque vocat. **2** de quo consultus, an esset
tempora maturae visurus longa senectae,
fatidicus vates 'si se non noverit' inquit.
3 vana diu visa est vox auguris: exitus illam
resque probat letique genus novitasque furoris.
4 namque ter ad quinos unum Cephisius annum
addiderat poteratque puer iuvenisque videri:
multi illum iuvenes, multae cupiere puellae;
sed fuit in tenera tam dura superbia forma,
nulli illum iuvenes, nullae tetigere puellae.
5 aspicit hunc trepidos agitantem in retia cervos
vocalis nymphe, quae nec reticere loquenti
nec prior ipsa loqui didicit, resonabilis Echo.

6 Corpus adhuc Echo, non vox erat et tamen usum
garrula non alium, quam nunc habet, oris habebat,
reddere de multis ut verba novissima posset.
7 fecerat hoc Iuno, quia, cum deprendere posset
sub Iove saepe suo nymphas in monte iacentis,
illa deam longo prudens sermone tenebat,
dum fugerent nymphae. **8** postquam hoc Saturnia sensit,
'huius' ait 'linguae, qua sum delusa, potestas
parva tibi dabitur vocisque brevissimus usus,'
reque minas firmat. **9** tantum haec in fine loquendi
ingeminat voces auditaque verba reportat.
10 ergo ubi Narcissum per devia rura vagantem
vidit et incaluit, sequitur vestigia furtim,
quoque magis sequitur, flamma propiore calescit,
non aliter quam cum summis circumlita taedis
admotas rapiunt vivacia sulphura flammas.
11 o quotiens voluit blandis accedere dictis
et mollis adhibere preces! natura repugnat
nec sinit, incipiat, sed, quod sinit, illa parata est
exspectare sonos, ad quos sua verba remittat.

1 Being Most famous throughout all of the Aonian cities,
Tiresias always gave perfectly accurate predictions to those asking him
about their fate;
first to test the truth of his words and voices was gloomy Liriope,
whom once Cephisus the river god had raped,
grasped her in his winding waters and taken her by force:
From her full womb, the most beautiful of nymphs had given birth to a
child, whom one was able to fall in love with him already, he is called
Narcissus.
2 Being consulted about, whether he would have a long life to mature
old age, the prophetic prophet said 'if he does not recognize himself'.
3 For a long time the voice of the augur was seen as empty, the
outcome and the cause of his death and strangeness of his madness
were proven.
4 For one year after the son of Cephisus had become fifteen
and might be seen as a boy and youth:
many young men and many girls desired him;
but he was held in a form of arrogance so intense,
that none of the young men or girls was able to grasp him.
5 Echo the answering talkative nymph, who neither kept quiet speaking
nor she learned to speak first, caught site of this man
chasing frightened deers into his hunting net.

6 Echo was still a body then, not a voice and however,
even though she was talkative, she could only speak as now
she was only able to repeat the very last words of another.
7 Juno made her like this, because, when she was often able to catch the
nymphs lying under Jupiter on the mountain, she knowingly
held the goddess in long conversations, while the nymphs fled.
8 Afterwards when Juno realized this,
she says, 'with this tongue, which has deluded me,
you will be given less power and the briefest use of your voice,'
and she did what she threatened.
9 Echo only reports the things last spoken and repeats the words she
hears.
10 Therefore when she sees Narcissus wondering
through the lonely countryside and falls in love, she follows him
furtively, the more she follows, the nearer she is inflamed with love,
no differently than when lively sulfur having been smeared
at the top of the touch seizes the flame brought near.
11 O how often she wanted to approach with charming words,
and to use gentle prayers! nature prevents nor allows her to begin, but
she is ready for what nature permits, to wait for sound to which she
sends back his own words.

12 forte puer comitum seductus ab agmine fido
dixerat: 'ecquis adest?' et 'adest' responderat Echo.
13 hic stupet, utque aciem partes dimittit in omnis,
voce 'veni!' magna clamat: vocat illa vocantem.
14 respicit et rursus nullo veniente 'quid' inquit
'me fugis?' et totidem, quot dixit, verba recepit.
15 perstat et alternae deceptus imagine vocis
'huc coeamus' ait, nullique libentius umquam
responsura sono 'coeamus' rettulit Echo
et verbis favet ipsa suis egressaque silva
ibat, ut iniceret sperato bracchia collo;
ille fugit fugiensque 'manus conplexibus aufer!
ante' ait 'emoriar, quam sit tibi copia nostri';
rettulit illa nihil nisi 'sit tibi copia nostri!'
spreta latet silvis pudibundaque frondibus ora
protegit et solis ex illo vivit in antris;
sed tamen haeret amor crescitque dolore repulsae;
extenuant vigiles corpus miserabile curae
adducitque cutem macies et in aera sucus
corporis omnis abit; vox tantum atque ossa supersunt:
vox manet, ossa ferunt lapidis traxisse figuram.
16 inde latet silvis nulloque in monte videtur,
omnibus auditur: sonus est, qui vivit in illa.

17 Sic hanc, sic alias undis aut montibus ortas
luserat hic nymphas, sic coetus ante viriles;
inde manus aliquis despectus ad aethera tollens
'sic amet ipse licet, sic non potiatur amato!'
dixerat: adsensit precibus Rhamnusia iustis.
18 fons erat inlimis, nitidis argenteus undis,
quem neque pastores neque pastae monte capellae
contigerant aliudve pecus, quem nulla volucris
nec fera turbarat nec lapsus ab arbore ramus;
gramen erat circa, quod proximus umor alebat,
silvaque sole locum passura tepescere nullo.
19 hic puer et studio venandi lassus et aestu
procubuit faciemque loci fontemque secutus,
dumque sitim sedare cupit, sitis altera crevit,
dumque bibit, visae correptus imagine formae
spem sine corpore amat, corpus putat esse, quod umbra est.
20 adstupet ipse sibi vultuque inmotus eodem
haeret, ut e Pario formatum marmore signum;

12 By chance the boy separated with his faithful column of men
had said 'is anyone present?' and Echo had said 'present'
he is astonished, as he sends glances in all directions,
with a great voice he shouts 'come'; called the following call.
13 He looked back and with no one coming he said
'why are you fleeing from me?' and the same number,
of words he said, the same number of words he received.
14 he persists having been tricked with the vision of another voice
'Let's meet here together' he said, no gladly than ever to reply to sound
Echo replied 'meet here together' and she supports her words by
coming out of the woods so that she hopes to throw her arms around
his neck; he flees from her and fleeing he says ' take away these
embracing hands! may I die before what's mine is yours';
She replied nothing except "what's mine is yours!'
Lying hidden in the woods having been reject and embarrassed
she covers her face with leaves and from then she lives in lonely caves;
but however, she clings to her love grows grief of rejection;
Her sleepless troubles weaken her pitiful body
and leads to thinning of her skin, and all of her body
goes away into moist in air; a voice and only bones remain:
a voice remains, some say her bones were dragged into the shape of
stones.
15 Ever since she lies hidden in the forest and was never seen in the
mountain.
16 She is heard by all: it is the sound, that lives in her.

17 He rejected her, just as he played the nymphs having been born
in the rivers or mountains, just as before he rejected a ground of men;
then one of those who had been despised, lifting his hand to the sky
said 'thus permit him to love himself, thus don't let him attain what he
loves!': Rhamnusia approved this righteous prayer.
18 There was a clear spring, with silvery shining waves, which had not
been disturbed by birds nor wild animals nor fallen branches of trees;
around there was grass, which was nourished by the proximate
moisture,
and the forest prevented the sun from warming up the place.
19 Here the boy tired out by his enthusiasm for hunting and by the heat
lay down attracted by both the appearance of the place and the spring,
and while he desired to quench his thirst, another thirst grew, and while
he was drinking,
captivated by the reflection he saw, he loves the bodiless dream,
he thinks that, which is only a shadow, is a body.
20 He is astonished by himself and clinging motionless with a fixed
expression, like a standard shaped from Parian marble;

spectat humi positus geminum, sua lumina, sidus
et dignos Baccho, dignos et Apolline crines
inpubesque genas et eburnea colla decusque
oris et in niveo mixtum candore ruborem,
cunctaque miratur, quibus est mirabilis ipse:
se cupit inprudens et, qui probat, ipse probatur,
dumque petit, petitur, pariterque accendit et ardet.
21 inrita fallaci quotiens dedit oscula fonti,
in mediis quotiens visum captantia collum
bracchia mersit aquis nec se deprendit in illis!
quid videat, nescit; sed quod videt, uritur illo,
atque oculos idem, qui decipit, incitat error.
22 credule, quid frustra simulacra fugacia captas?
quod petis, est nusquam; quod amas, avertere, perdes!
ista repercussae, quam cernis, imaginis umbra est:
nil habet ista sui; tecum venitque manetque;
tecum discedet, si tu discedere possis!

23 Non illum Cereris, non illum cura quietis
abstrahere inde potest, sed opaca fusus in herba
spectat inexpleto mendacem lumine formam
perque oculos perit ipse suos; paulumque levatus
ad circumstantes tendens sua bracchia silvas
'ecquis, io silvae, crudelius' inquit 'amavit?
scitis enim et multis latebra opportuna fuistis.
24 ecquem, cum vestrae tot agantur saecula vitae,
qui sic tabuerit, longo meministis in aevo?
et placet et video; sed quod videoque placetque,
non tamen invenio' tantus tenet error amantem
'quoque magis doleam, nec nos mare separat ingens
nec via nec montes nec clausis moenia portis;
exigua prohibemur aqua! cupit ipse teneri:
nam quotiens liquidis porreximus oscula lymphis,
hic totiens ad me resupino nititur ore.
25 posse putes tangi: minimum est, quod amantibus obstat.
26 quisquis es, huc exi! quid me, puer unice, fallis
quove petitus abis?
certe nec forma nec aetas
est mea, quam fugias, et amarunt me quoque nymphae!
spem mihi nescio quam vultu promittis amico,
cumque ego porrexi tibi bracchia, porrigis ultro,
cum risi, adrides; lacrimas quoque saepe notavi
me lacrimante tuas; nutu quoque signa remittis
et, quantum motu formosi suspicor oris,
verba refers aures non pervenientia nostras!

lying on the ground he contemplates at twin stars, his own eyes, and his
hair, worthy of Bacchus and the hair worthy of Apollo,
and his youthful cheeks and ivory-neck and beauty
of his face and the blush mixed with snow-white radiance,
and he admires everything for which he himself is admired.
21 Unknowingly he desires himself and, the one who wants, is himself is
wanted, and while he seeks, he is sought, and equally he inflames and is
inflamed.
22 How often did he give futile kisses to the deceitful fountain,
How often did he submerge his arms in the water trying to catch the
neck that he saw but did not catch himself in them!
He does not know what he sees, but he is inflamed seeing the illusion,
and the same illusion that deceives his eyes leads him on.
23 fool, why are you capturing a fleeting image in vain?
what you seek is nowhere; turn away, what you love, that reflection is
lost, what you perceive, is the shadow of an image:
nothing you have is in it; it comes with you and stays with you;
it leaves with you, if you are able to leave!

Then he is able to withdraw from that of Ceres, or care for anything
else, but stretched out on the shaded grass he watches at that illusion
with unsated eyes, and he is lost in his own eyes; and having risen
a little extending his arms to the surround woods he said
"Is there anyone, oh trees, who loved more cruelly than me?
for you know and you have been the opportune hiding place of many.
24 Is there anyone, in your life that is so long
that you remember in eras, who wastes away thus?
and I see he pleases me; but what I see and pleases me,
I however cannot find" loving holds an error so great
"likewise I am hurt more, that neither great seas
nor roads nor mountains nor walls with enclosed doors separate us;
we are stopped by a small pond! He himself desires to be held:
for how often we have extended kiss by the water,
I bend down as often as he presses forward his lips to me.
25 you think he is able to be touched: it is the smallest thing, which
stops our love.
26 whoever you are, come here! Why, unique boy,
do you vanish when you have been sought by me?
Surely it is neither my form nor age
that you flee from, and even nymphs had loved me!
You promised me unknown hope with your loving gaze,
and when I offered my arms to you, you offered yours,
when I smiled, you smile; I even often observe your tears when I weep;
you even send back my gesture of nodding and,
from the movement of your beautiful mouth, I suspect you reply with
words that do not reach my ears!

iste ego sum: sensi, nec me mea fallit imago;
uror amore mei: flammas moveoque feroque.
27 quid faciam? roger anne rogem? quid deinde rogabo?
quod cupio mecum est: inopem me copia fecit.
28 o utinam a nostro secedere corpore possem!
votum in amante novum, vellem, quod amamus, abesset.
29 iamque dolor vires adimit, nec tempora vitae
longa meae superant, primoque exstinguor in aevo.
30 nec mihi mors gravis est posituro morte dolores,
hic, qui diligitur, vellem diuturnior esset;
nunc duo concordes anima moriemur in una.'

31 Dixit et ad faciem rediit male sanus eandem
et lacrimis turbavit aquas, obscuraque moto
reddita forma lacu est; quam cum vidisset abire,
'quo refugis? remane nec me, crudelis, amantem
desere!' clamavit; 'liceat, quod tangere non est,
adspicere et misero praebere alimenta furori!'
dumque dolet, summa vestem deduxit ab ora
nudaque marmoreis percussit pectora palmis.
32 pectora traxerunt roseum percussa ruborem,
non aliter quam poma solent, quae candida parte,
parte rubent, aut ut variis solet uva racemis
ducere purpureum nondum matura colorem.
33 quae simul adspexit liquefacta rursus in unda,
non tulit ulterius, sed ut intabescere flavae
igne levi cerae matutinaeque pruinae
sole tepente solent, sic attenuatus amore
liquitur et tecto paulatim carpitur igni;
et neque iam color est mixto candore rubori,
nec vigor et vires et quae modo visa placebant,
nec corpus remanet, quondam quod amaverat Echo.
34 quae tamen ut vidit, quamvis irata memorque,
indoluit, quotiensque puer miserabilis 'eheu'
dixerat, haec resonis iterabat vocibus 'eheu';
cumque suos manibus percusserat ille lacertos,
haec quoque reddebat sonitum plangoris eundem.
35 ultima vox solitam fuit haec spectantis in undam:
'heu frustra dilecte puer!' totidemque remisit
verba locus, dictoque vale 'vale' inquit et Echo.
36 ille caput viridi fessum submisit in herba,
lumina mors clausit domini mirantia formam:
tum quoque se, postquam est inferna sede receptus,

I am in you, I felt it, neither does my image deceive me;
I am burning with love for myself: I aroused the fire and I suffer it.
27 What do I do? Should I ask or be asked? Then what will I ask for?
what I want is with me: my riches made me poor.
28 Oh if only I could separate from self from me!
a strange prayer for a lover, I wished, what we love, is not here.
29 And now sorrow steals strength, neither remain
a long time of my life, and I am quenched in the prime of age.
30 neither is death unpleasant to me, laying down my sorrows in death,
he, who is loved, I wish to be long last;
now the two of us will die, our souls as one in harmony."
31 He said and he returned to the same reflection with a sick mind
and his tears unsettles the water, and the image is obscured
in the rippling pool; when he saw it disappear,
he shouted "where are you fleeing to? Stay with me, cruel one, don't
abandon the man that love you! I am allowed to look at what I cannot
touch,
and offer food for my miserable madness!"
and while he laments, he pulls his tunic over his head
and stripped naked he struck his chests with hands of marble.
32 His chests turn pink redness with each strike,
no different from an apple, which is part shining white,
part red, or just as unripe grapes in various clusters
taking a purple color.
33 Who at the same time he looked on the clear water again,
but he could not endure any longer, just as yellow wax
is accustomed to melt with a gentle fire
and the morning frost is accustomed to melt with the warming sun,
in this way weakened with love
he wastes away and gradually he is consumed by the hidden fire;
and neither his rosy white complexion now glows,
nor the energy and strength and that form which was so pleasing to be
seen, there remained a body, which Echo once had loved.
34 However when she saw him, although angry remembering what
happened she felt sorry,
how often the boy says 'alas' pitifully
she repeated with her voice echoing word 'alas';
And since his hands had struck at his arm,
Echo also gave back the same sound of the grief.
35 These were the last words of the one looking into the familiar water:
'Alas in vain beloved boy!' and she sent back the same number of words
to him, and having said farewell, Echo said 'farewell'.
36 He laid down his tired head on the green grass,
death closed the lights admiring the beauty of their master:
then after he was received into the underworld,

in Stygia spectabat aqua. **37** planxere sorores
naides et sectos fratri posuere capillos,
planxerunt dryades; plangentibus adsonat Echo.
38 iamque rogum quassasque faces feretrumque parabant:
nusquam corpus erat; croceum pro corpore florem
inveniunt foliis medium cingentibus albis.

he received a seat where he watches himself in the waters of the river Styx.

37 The Naiads weeping had cut their hair and placed them for their brother, the Dryads wailed; Echo echoes their wails.

38 And now they were preparing the funeral bier, shaking the torches: nowhere was the body; in return for his body, they find a yellow flower with white petals surrounding its middle.

PARIS TO HELEN
OVID'S HERIODES XVI

1 Hanc tibi Priamides mitto, Ledaea, salutem,
  quae tribui sola te mihi dante potest.

2 eloquar, an flammae non est opus indice notae,
  et plus quam vellem, iam meus extat amor?

3 ille quidem lateat malim, dum tempora dentur
  laetitiae mixtos non habitura metus.

4 sed male dissimulo; quis enim celaverit ignem,
  lumine qui semper proditur ipse suo?

5 si tamen expectas, vocem quoque rebus ut addam:
  uror—habes animi nuntia verba mei.

6 parce, precor, fasso, nec vultu cetera duro
  perlege, sed formae conveniente tuae.

7 iamdudum gratum est, quod epistula nostra recepta
  spem facit, hoc recipi me quoque posse modo.

8 quae rata sit; nec te frustra promiserit, opto,
  hoc mihi quae suasit, mater Amoris, iter.

9 namque ego divino monitu—ne nescia pecces—
  advehor et coepto non leve numen adest.

10 praemia magna quidem, sed non indebita posco:
  pollicita est thalamo te Cytherea meo.

11 hac duce Sigeo dubias a litore feci
  longa Phereclea per freta puppe vias.

12 illa dedit faciles auras ventosque secundos—
  in mare nimirum ius habet orta mari.

13 perstet et ut pelagi, sic pectoris adiuvet aestum,
  deferat in portus et mea vota suos.

14 attulimus flammas, non hic invenimus, illas.

15 hae mihi tam longae causa fuere viae.

16 nam neque tristis hiems neque nos huc appulit error;
  Taenaris est classi terra petita meae.

17 nec me crede fretum merces portante carina
  findere—quas habeo, di tueantur opes.

18 nec venio Graias veluti spectator ad urbes;
  oppida sunt regni divitiora mei.

19 te peto, quam pepigit lecto Venus aurea nostro;
  te prius optavi quam mihi nota fores.

20 ante tuos animo vidi quam lumine vultus;
  prima tulit vulnus nuntia fama tui.

21 nec tamen est mirum, si sicut oportuit arcu,
  missilibus telis eminus ictus amo.

22 sic placuit fatis; quae ne convellere temptes,
  accipe cum vera dicta relata fide.

1 Daughter of Leda, I son of Priam send you prosperity,
which I wish that only you can grant me.
2 Should I speak plainly, or is there no need to signal my known love,
and now my love is projected, do I receive more of my desire?
3 In fact I wish to hide it, until a time is given
where fear is not mixed with joy.
4 but I dissimulate badly; for who can hide a fire,
which always reveals itself with its own light?
5 If however you expect my love, I will add my thoughts on the matter:
I am inflamed with love – you have the words that announce my soul.
6 forgive my for my confession, I beg you, don't read the rest
with hard expression, but harmonize it with your beauty.
7 I have been grateful long since, when you accepted my letter
it gave me hope, this way you would also accept me.
8 Let it be certain; I hope, that you are not promised to me in vain,
by the mother of Love, who has urged me to take this journey.
9 For the goddess advises me – you cannot sin with ignorance -
I will be with you and the will of the goddess is with me.
10 The reward I demand is great in deed, but one owed to me:
as Venus promised you to my bed.
11 Led by her I left the Sigean shores with an undecided mind
making my way through the vast seas to the Phereclean ship.
12 she brought a gentle breeze and a second wind –
born from the sea she without a doubt commands the seas.
13 May she preserve further, thus she help the passion of my heart,
she brings me into port and my promise to you.
14 my flame had been carried forth, I did not find them here.
15 They have been the reason of my journey so long.
16 For no foul storm nor erroneous journey led us here;
my fleet sought the land of Sparta.
17 Nor I believe I divided the sea with ships carrying merchandise –
I have all these things, the gods bless me with wealth.
18 Nor I came as a tourist to the Greek cities;
my kingdom is filled with towns more divine.
19 I seek you, whom glamorous Venus chose and promised me;
I wished for you before you were known to me.
20 Before I saw you with my eyes you were in my mind;
fame brought the first message of your beauty.
21 Nor is it a miracle, just like ordered by a bow,
an arrow strikes from afar as I am with love.
22 Thus destiny is satisfied, which you cannot try to defeat,
accept with a speech of true words the telling of your faith.

23 matris adhuc utero partu remorante tenebar;
    iam gravidus iusto pondere venter erat.
24 illa sibi ingentem visa est sub imagine somni
    flammiferam pleno reddere ventre facem.
25 territa consurgit metuendaque noctis opacae
    visa seni Priamo, vatibus ille refert.
26 arsurum Paridis vates canit Ilion igni—
    pectoris, ut nunc est, fax fuit illa mei.
27 forma vigorque animi, quamvis de plebe videbar,
    indicium tectae nobilitatis erat.
28 est locus in mediis nemorosae vallibus Idae
    devius et piceis ilicibusque frequens,
qui nec ovis placidae nec amantis saxa capellae
    nec patulo tardae carpitur ore bovis;
hinc ego Dardaniae muros excelsaque tecta
    et freta prospiciens arbore nixus eram—
ecce, pedum pulsu visa est mihi terra moveri—
    vera loquar veri vix habitura fidem—
constitit ante oculos actus velocibus alis
    Atlantis magni Pleionesque nepos—
fas vidisse fuit, fas sit mihi visa referre—
    inque dei digitis aurea virga fuit.
29 tresque simul divae, Venus et cum Pallade Iuno,
    graminibus teneros inposuere pedes.
30 obstupui, gelidusque comas erexerat horror,
    cum mihi 'pone metum!' nuntius ales ait:
'arbiter es formae; certamina siste dearum,
    vincere quae forma digna sit una duas.'
31 neve recusarem, verbis Iovis imperat et se
    protinus aetheria tollit in astra via.
32 mens mea convaluit, subitoque audacia venit
    nec timui vultu quamque notare meo.
33 vincere erant omnes dignae iudexque querebar
    non omnes causam vincere posse suam.
34 sed tamen ex illis iam tunc magis una placebat,
    hanc esse ut scires, unde movetur amor.
35 tantaque vincendi cura est; ingentibus ardent
    iudicium donis sollicitare meum.
36 regna Iovis coniunx, virtutem filia iactat;
    ipse potens dubito fortis an esse velim.
37 dulce Venus risit; 'nec te, Pari, munera tangant
    utraque suspensi plena timoris,' ait;
'nos dabimus, quod ames, et pulchrae filia Ledae
    ibit in amplexus pulchrior illa tuos.'
38 dixit, et ex aequo donis formaque probata
    victorem caelo rettulit illa pedem.

23 while still held in the womb of my mother delaying my birth;
now deservedly pregnant with a grave burden.
24 she seems to be under a mysterious dream
where she delivers flaming torches from her pregnant belly.
25 she woke up terrified and the spoke of the fearful vision
of the dark night to old Priam, he turns to his seers
26 A prophet foretold that Troy was about to be burnt with Paris' fire –
such as there is now, the torch in my heart.
27 The beauty and vigor of my soul, though I seem to be a commoner,
were evidence of my hidden nobility.
28 There is a place in the midst of the wooded Idan alleys
desolated and filled pines and holm-oaks,
where neither placid sheep nor she-goats who love rocks
nor slow oxen even with open mouths will graze;
Here I was leaning again a true gazing down
on the walls and lofty roofs of Troy and the sea –
Behold, the ground seem to move with my step –
I speak the true scarcely having faith it to be true –
Before my eyes appeared carried by his swift wings –
The grandson (Mercury)of mighty Atlas and Pleione –
it was my destiny to see it, let is be right to recount what I saw –
I say there was a golden staff in the gods fingers.
29 And at the same time three gods, Venus, Pallas, and Juno,
set there soft feet on the grass.
30 I was starstruck, and my hair rose with an icy chill,
when the winged messenger said to me: 'put behind your fear
you are an arbiter of beauty; end the goddess's contest,
whose beauty is worthy of conquering the other twos.'
31 I did not refuse, he ordered me in the name of Jupiter and he
immediately rose into the stars the road to heaven.
32 My spirit recovered, and a sudden courage came
I was not afraid to observe each of their appearances.
33 All were worthy of victory and being juror I complained
none of all their cases was able to win.
34 But now one out of them pleased me more,
she to be known as, from where love was set in motion.
35 And they all wanted to win so much; they were so consumed
that they tempted my judgement with extraordinary gifts.
36 Jupiter's wife spoke about kingdoms, her daughter about valor;
I would like to be able to think about power or valor.
37 Sweet Venus laughed; 'Paris don't let either reward bewitch you
and they are full of anxious fear,' she said;
'I will give you, what you love, the more daughter of beautiful Leda
who is more beautiful will go into your arms.'
38 And having approved her beauty and gift justly
victorious she retraced her steps into the sky.

39 interea, credo, versis ad prospera fatis
   regius agnoscor per rata signa puer.
40 laeta domus nato per tempora longa recepto,
   addit et ad festos hunc quoque Troia diem.
41 utque ego te cupio, sic me cupiere puellae;
   multarum votum sola tenere potes.
42 nec tantum regum natae petiere ducumque,
   sed nymphis etiam curaque amorque fui.
43 quas super Oenonen facies mutarer in orbem
   nec Priamo est a te dignior ulla nurus.
44 sed mihi cunctarum subeunt fastidia, postquam
   coniugii spes est, Tyndari, facta tui.
45 te vigilans oculis, animo te nocte videbam,
   lumina cum placido victa sopore iacent.
46 quid facies praesens, quae nondum visa placebas?
   ardebam, quamvis hic procul ignis erat.
47 nec potui debere mihi spem longius istam,
   caerulea peterem quin mea vota via.
48 Troia caeduntur Phrygia pineta securi
   quaeque erat aequoreis utilis arbor aquis;
ardua proceris spoliantur Gargara silvis,
   innumerasque mihi longa dat Ida trabes.
49 fundatura citas flectuntur robora naves
   texitur et costis panda carina suis.
50 addimus antennas et vela sequentia malo
   accipit et pictos puppis adunca deos;
qua tamen ipse vehor, comitata Cupidine parvo
   sponsor coniugii stat dea picta sui.
51 imposita est factae postquam manus ultima classi,
   protinus Aegaeis ire lubebat aquis.
52 at pater et genetrix inhibent mea vota rogando
   propositumque pia voce morantur iter;
et soror effusis ut erat Cassandra capillis,
   cum vellent nostrae iam dare vela rates,
'quo ruis?' exclamat, 'referes incendia tecum!
   quanta per has nescis flamma petatur aquas!'
vera fuit vates; dictos invenimus ignes
   et ferus in molli pectore flagrat amor.
53 portubus egredior ventisque ferentibus usus
   applicor in terras, Oebali nympha, tuas.
54 excipit hospitio vir me tuus: hoc quoque factum
   non sine consilio numinibusque deum.
55 ille quidem ostendit, quidquid Lacedaemone tota
   ostendi dignum conspicuumque fuit;
sed mihi laudatam cupienti cernere formam
   lumina nil aliud quo caperentur erat.

39 meanwhile, I believe, the fates turned to my prosperity
I was acknowledged as the son of a king through established signs.
40 A house made happy though the acceptance of a long lost son,
and because of this Troy acquire a day of festival.
41 As much as I want you, girls desire me too;
you along are able to hold the will of many.
42 Not only do daughters of kings and dukes seek me,
but I am even cared for and loved by nymphs.
43 Whose beauty in the world was more than Oenone's
after you no one is worthy of being the daughter in law of Priam.
44 but they have all come to me with disgust, after
I hope to make you, Helen, my wife.
45 awake my eyes see you, I was see you in my mind at night
my drowsy eyes lie conquered by tranquil sleep.
46 How is your beauty, which you have not allowed me to see, be in my
mind? I am inflamed, though the fire was far away from me.
47 Neither am I able to bound any longer my hope of you,
I seek out my desire with a dark-blue journey.
48 The Trojan pine woods felled by a Phrygian axe
each tree useful for waves of the sea;
tall forests were stripped from lofty Mt. Gargaron
and far-stretched Mt. Ida gave countless amounts of timber to me.
49 Oak trees were curved as foundation for my swift ships
and the curved keel is woven into the ribbed sides
50 We add the yards and sails hanging onto the mast
and hooked sterns received images of gods;
the one who endorsed me, with her small son Cupid
an ornated goddess stands as surety of his union.
51 After the last hand had worked on the fleet,
immediately I desire to sail the Aegean seas.
52 But my father and mother prevent my desire with prayed
and good intentions they voiced for me to delay my journey;
and my sister Cassandra just as she is with her hair loose,
when our ships were now eager to spread the sail,
cried 'whereto do you sail? You will bring destruction back with you!
you do not know how great the flame you seek over these waters!'
there was truth in her oracle; I found the spoken fires
and I blazed with fierce love in my yielding heart.
53 But I left the harbor and using the winds carrying me
I landed on your kingdom, nymph of Oebalus.
54 Your husband welcomes me as a guest: this too was done
not without the divine will and counsel of the gods
55 In fact he showed me, whatever the in the whole of Sparta
was worthy and distinguished enough to be shown to me;
but I desire to see you praised beauty
and there was nothing else that could capture my eyes.

56 ut vidi, obstipui praecordiaque intima sensi
　　attonitus curis intumuisse novis.
57 his similes vultus, quantum reminiscor, habebat,
　　venit in arbitrium cum Cytherea meum.
58 si tu venisses pariter certamen in illud,
　　in dubium Veneris palma futura fuit.
59 magna quidem de te rumor praeconia fecit,
　　nullaque de facie nescia terra tua est;
nec tibi par usquam Phrygia nec solis ab ortu
　　inter formosas altera nomen habet!
credis et hoc nobis?—minor est tua gloria vero
　　famaque de forma paene maligna tua est.
60 plus hic invenio, quam quod promiserat illa,
　　et tua materia gloria victa sua est.
61 ergo arsit merito, qui noverat omnia, Theseus,
　　et visa es tanto digna rapina viro,
more tuae gentis nitida dum nuda palaestra
　　ludis et es nudis femina mixta viris.
62 quod rapuit, laudo; miror quod reddidit umquam.
63　tam bona constanter praeda tenenda fuit.
64 ante recessisset caput hoc cervice cruenta,
　　quam tu de thalamis abstraherere meis.
65 tene manus umquam nostrae dimittere vellent?
　　tene meo paterer vivus abire sinu?
si reddenda fores, aliquid tamen ante tulissem
　　nec Venus ex toto nostra fuisset iners.
66 vel mihi virginitas esset libata vel illud
　　quod poterat salva virginitate rapi.
67 da modo te, quae sit Paridis constantia nosces:
　　flamma rogi flammas finiet una meas.
68 praeposui regnis ego te, quae maxima quondam
　　pollicita est nobis nupta sororque Iovis,
dumque tuo possem circumdare bracchia collo,
　　contempta est virtus Pallade dante mihi.
69 nec piget aut umquam stulte legisse videbor;
　　permanet in voto mens mea firma suo.
70 spem modo ne nostram fieri patiare caducam,
　　deprecor, o tanto digna labore peti!
non ego coniugium generosae degener opto,
　　nec mea, crede mihi, turpiter uxor eris.
71 Pliada, si quaeres, in nostra gente Iovemque
　　invenies, medios ut taceamus avos.
72 sceptra parens Asiae, qua nulla beatior ora est,
　　finibus inmensis vix obeunda, tenet.
73 innumeras urbes atque aurea tecta videbis
　　quaeque suos dicas templa decere deos.

56 As I saw you, I was stunned and I felt
the innermost of my chest thunderstruck by new cares rising.
57 She had similar appearances as I remember,
When Venus came to my judgement.
58 If you came together in that contest,
Venus would have only been barely victorious.
59 The rumor has indeed made great advertising for you
that no country does not know your beauty;
nowhere in Phrygia can equal your beauty nor from the rising Sun
no other beautiful woman has a name like yours!
will you believe me when I say this? – your glory is less than the truth
for fame has always diminished your beauty.
60 I find more here, than that which the goddess promised me,
and your reality is more than your glory.
61 As a result Theseus, who knew everything, deserves to be burned,
and you were seen as plunder worthy for such a hero,
when you are in the wrestling ring naked by your people's customs
a sport with naked women mixing with naked men.
62 I praise that he took you; I am amazed that he ever returned you.
63 He should firmly hold spoils so great.
64 this head has been severed from a bloody nape,
before you are taken away from my bed.
65 Would my hands ever want to send you away?
would I let you leave my side while alive?
if you must be returned, however before I have been brought anything
neither Venus was entirely idle.
66 And I would taste your virginity or
I would take what I can with your virginity safe.
67 Only give yourself, and you will know of Paris' constancy:
the fire of the funeral pyre alone can end my burning passion.
68 I preferred you to kingdom, which the greatest
was promised to me by the wife and sister of Jupiter,
and while I can surround you neck with my arms,
the power of Pallas' offering is despicable to me.
69 Neither it pains me nor anting I am seen to choose is foolish;
my conscience remains firm in devotion for you.
70 My only prayer, is that you don't allow my hope suffer death,
O I seek something worthy of so much labour!
I'm not a low-born wishing for a wife of nobility,
neither will it be ugly, believe me, to be my wife.
71 A Pleiad, if you will seek for, you will find in our line
a Jupiter, it's inconsiderate to saying nothing of my ancestors.
72 My father holds the staff of Asia, and nowhere is more prosperous,
with immense borders that have been hardly reached.
73 you will see countless cities and golden dwellings
and temples that you would say are suitable for gods.

74 Ilion adspicies firmataque turribus altis
    moenia, Phoebeae structa canore lyrae.
75 quid tibi de turba narrem numeroque virorum?
    vix populum tellus sustinet illa suum.
76 occurrent denso tibi Troades agmine matres
    nec capient Phrygias atria nostra nurus.
77 o quotiens dices: 'quam pauper Achaia nostra est!'
    una domus quaevis urbis habebit opes.
78 nec mihi fas fuerit Sparten contemnere vestram:
    in qua tu nata es, terra beata mihi est.
79 parca sed est Sparte, tu cultu divite digna;
    ad talem formam non facit iste locus.
80 hanc faciem largis sine fine paratibus uti
    deliciisque decet luxuriare novis.
81 cum videas cultus nostra de gente virorum,
    qualem Dardanias credis habere nurus?
da modo te facilem nec dedignare maritum,
    rure Therapnaeo nata puella, Phrygem.
82 Phryx erat et nostro genitus de sanguine, qui nunc
    cum dis potando nectare miscet aquas.
83 Phryx erat Aurorae coniunx, tamen abstulit illum
    extremum noctis quae dea finit iter.
84 Phryx etiam Anchises, volucrum cui mater Amorum
    gaudet in Idaeis concubuisse iugis.
85 nec, puto, conlatis forma Menelaus et annis
    iudice te nobis anteferendus erit.
86 non dabimus certe socerum tibi clara fugantem
    lumina, qui trepidos a dape vertat equos;
nec Priamo pater est soceri de caede cruentus
    et qui Myrtoas crimine signat aquas;
nec proavo Stygia nostro captantur in unda
    poma, nec in mediis quaeritur umor aquis.
87 quid tamen hoc refert, si te tenet ortus ab illis?
    cogitur huic domui Iuppiter esse socer.
88 heu facinus! totis indignus noctibus ille
    te tenet amplexu perfruiturque tuo;
at mihi conspiceris posita vix denique mensa
    multaque quae laedant hoc quoque tempus habet.
89 hostibus eveniant convivia talia nostris,
    experior posito qualia saepe mero.
90 paenitet hospitii, cum me spectante lacertos
    imponit collo rusticus iste tuo.
91 rumpor et invideo—quid ni tamen omnia narrem?—
    membra superiecta cum tua veste fovet.
92 oscula cum vero coram non dura daretis,
    ante oculos posui pocula sumpta meos;

74 You will see Troy and its tall fortified towers
on the walls, built by the song of Apollo's lyre.
75 What can I tell you about the crowds and number of heroes?
the earth can hardly sustain such a population.
76 In dense lines the Trojan women will rush to meet you
neither will our halls contain the daughters of Phrygia.
77 O how often do you say "how poor is our Achaia!"
one house no matter which will show a city's wealth.
78 Neither it was proper for me to disparage your Sparta:
in where you were born, the land is rich for me.
79 but Sparta is small, you are worthy of a wealthy culture;
this place is not made for such beauty.
80 That beauty is made to enjoy copious adornments without end
and it is proper to have new luxuries for you in abundance.
81 When you see the culture of the men of our race,
what do you think the daughters of Phrygia have?
Only if you do not easily reject a Phrygian husband,
a girl born in the countryside of Therapnae.
82 It was a Phrygian and born of our blood, who now
mixes water with the nectar which is to be drunk by gods.
83 Aurora's husband it was a Phrygian, however she carried him away
the goddess who sets border for the journey of the night.
84 It is also a Phrygia Anchises, whom the mother of Winged Cupid
loves to sleep with on Mt. Ida's ridges.
85 Neither, I do think, Menelaus comparing our age and beauty
would prefer me even in your judgement
86 I will certainly not give you a father-in-law who chases away the clear
light of the sun, whom turned his terrified horses away from a feast;
neither is Priam bloodstained from the assassination of his father-in-law
and who marks the Myrtoan waters with his crimes;
nor do my ancestors catch in the Stygian waves
fruits, nor seek for water in the midst of water.
87 However what call to mind is, if one born from them holds you?
Jupiter is forced to be the father-in-law of this house.
88 Oh the crime! Through the nights that unworthy man
holds your embrace and enjoying you;
but I hardly see you when the tables are finally set
and many things that hurt me even this time has.
89 May our enemies befall to such feast as ours,
the kind that I often suffer when pure wine is placed.
90 I regret being a guest, when I see that arm
that boor placed around your neck
91 I am anger and I envy – but why should I not I tell you everything?–
when he covers your limbs with his robe so you are warm.
92 When you truly give him gentle kisses in my presence,
I place my cup in front of my eyes;

lumina demitto cum te tenet artius ille,
    crescit et invito lentus in ore cibus.
93 saepe dedi gemitus; et te, lasciva, notavi
    in gemitu risum non tenuisse meo.
94 saepe mero volui flammam compescere, at illa
    crevit, et ebrietas ignis in igne fuit.
95 multaque ne videam, versa cervice recumbo;
    sed revocas oculos protinus ipsa meos.
96 quid faciam, dubito; dolor est meus illa videre,
    sed dolor a facie maior abesse tua.
97 qua licet et possum, luctor celare furorem,
    sed tamen apparet dissimulatus amor.
98 nec tibi verba damus; sentis mea vulnera, sentis;
    atque utinam soli sint ea nota tibi.
99 a, quotiens lacrimis venientibus ora reflexi,
    ne causam fletus quaereret ille mei.
100 a, quotiens aliquem narravi potus amorem,
    ad vulnus referens singula verba tuos,
indiciumque mei ficto sub nomine feci;
    ille ego, si nescis, verus amator eram.
101 quin etiam ut possem verbis petulantius uti,
    non semel ebrietas est simulata mihi.
102 Prodita sunt, memini, tunica tua pectora laxa
    atque oculis aditum nuda dedere meis
pectora vel puris nivibus vel lacte tuamve
    complexo matrem candidiora Iove.
103 dum stupeo visis—nam pocula forte tenebam—
    tortilis a digitis excidit ansa meis.
104 oscula si natae dederas, ego protinus illa
    Hermiones tenero laetus ab ore tuli.
105 et modo cantabam veteres resupinus amores
    et modo per nutum signa tegenda dabam.
106 et comitum primas Clymenen Aethramque, tuarum
    ausus sum blandis nuper adire sonis;
quae mihi non aliud, quam formidare locutae
    orantis medias deseruere preces.
107 di facerent, pretium magni certaminis esses,
    teque suo posset victor habere toro,
ut tulit Hippomenes Schoeneida praemia cursus,
    venit ut in Phrygios Hippodamia sinus,
ut ferus Alcides Acheloia cornua fregit,
    dum petit amplexus, Deianira, tuos.
108 nostra per has leges audacia fortiter isset
    teque mei scires esse laboris opus.
109 nunc mihi nil superest nisi te, formosa, precari
    amplectique tuos, si patiare, pedes.

when he holds you firmly I close my eyes,
the food in my mouth becomes sticky and challenging.
93 I often let out a groan; and you, lustful girl, I noticed
you not able to hold back laughter at my groans.
94 I often wished to restrain my flame with wine, but my flame
grew, and drunkenness was a fire in fire.
95 And many times so I may not see you, I recline my turned neck;
but you immediately call back my eyes.
96 what I should do, I question; it is my pain to see you,
but it causes a greater pain for me to not see you.
97 As I can and might, I struggle to hide my passion,
but my concealed love is still visible.
98 Neither do I give you lies; you feel my wounds, you feel them;
and oh I hope that they are only known to you.
99 Ah, how often I turned away my face when tears came,
so that he does not ask the cause of my sorrow.
100 Ah, how often I told others tales of love when drunk,
echoing every single word to you my wound,
and I made my story fiction under another name;
I, if you were not aware, truly was the lover.
101 And moreover that I can use wanton words,
not once have I imitated my drunkenness.
102 They were exposed, I remember, your breasts released by your tunic
and gave my eyes an opportunity to you naked
breasts fairer than pure snow or milk
or Jove who embraced your mother.
103 When I am stunned gazing – for I held my cups strongly –
the twisted handle fell out from my fingers.
104 If you gave kisses to your daughter, I would instantly
steal them from Hermonie's tender lips.
105 And now lying on my back I sang about loves of old
and now through a nod I gave you secret.
106 And your best friends Clymene and Aethra, whom
I recently dared to approach with flattering speech
who said to me nothing else, but that they were afraid
leaving in the middle of my entreaties.
107 The gods should make, you to be the prize of a great contest,
and the victor can have you for his bed,
just like Hippomenes took Schoeney's daughter as a reward in a race
Hippodamia came to Phrygia's protection,
just as Alcides broke Achelous's rough horns
while he sought embraces from her, Deianira.
108 My courage had advanced boldly through these stipulations
and you would know to be the work of my labour.
109 Now I have nothing left for me to you, my beautiful, but to beg
and to embrace, if you allow it, your feet.

110 o decus, o praesens geminorum gloria fratrum,
　　o Iove digna viro, ni Iove nata fores,
aut ego Sigeos repetam te coniuge portus
　　aut hic Taenaria contegar exul humo!
non mea sunt summa leviter destricta sagitta
　　pectora; descendit vulnus ad ossa meum!
hoc mihi, nam repeto, fore ut a caeleste sagitta
　　figar, erat verax vaticinata soror.

111 parce datum fatis, Helene, contemnere amorem—
　　sic habeas faciles in tua vota deos.

112 multa quidem subeunt; sed coram ut plura loquamur,
　　excipe me lecto nocte silente tuo.

113 an pudet et metuis Venerem temerare maritam
　　castaque legitimi fallere iura tori?
a, nimium simplex Helene, ne rustica dicam,
　　hanc faciem culpa posse carere putas?
aut faciem mutes aut sis non dura, necesse est;
　　lis est cum forma magna pudicitiae.

114 Iuppiter his gaudet, gaudet Venus aurea furtis;
　　haec tibi nempe patrem furta dedere Iovem.

115 vix fieri, si sunt vires in semine amorum,
　　et Iovis et Ledae filia casta potes.

116 casta tamen tum sis, cum te mea Troia tenebit,
　　et tua sim quaeso crimina solus ego.

117 nunc ea peccemus quae corriget hora iugalis,
　　si modo promisit non mihi vana Venus.

118 sed tibi et hoc suadet rebus, non voce, maritus,
　　neve sui furtis hospitis obstet, abest.

119 non habuit tempus, quo Cresia regna videret
　　aptius—o mira calliditate virum!
'res, et ut Idaei mando tibi,' dixit iturus,
　　'curam pro nobis hospitis, uxor, agas.'
neglegis absentis, testor, mandata mariti;
　　cura tibi non est hospitis ulla tui.

120 huncine tu speras hominem sine pectore dotes
　　posse satis formae, Tyndari, nosse tuae?
falleris: ignorat, nec, si bona magna putaret,
　　quae tenet, externo crederet illa viro.

121 ut te nec mea vox nec te meus incitet ardor,
　　cogimur ipsius commoditate frui:
aut erimus stulti, sic ut superemus et ipsum,
　　si tam securum tempus abibit iners.

122 paene suis ad te manibus deducit amantem;
　　utere mandantis simplicitate viri!
sola iaces viduo tam longa nocte cubili;
　　in viduo iaceo solus et ipse toro.

110 O honour, O present glory of twin brethren,

O a woman worthy of Jove for a husband, if you were not his daughter,

or else I recall Sigeum's harbour with you my wife

or I am buried by Taenarian earth in exile!

my heart has not slightly been unsheathed by the arrow's point;

the wound has pierced to my bones!

This, for I now recall, to be transfixed by the heavenly arrow,

was what my truthful sister prophesised.

111 You scantily despise this love, Helen, given by fate–

so that the gods will have mercy to your prayers.

112 Indeed many things come to mind; but may we say more in person,

take me to your bed in the silent night.

113 Or are you afraid and ashamed to violate your married love

and to deceive the pure laws of lawful marriage bed?

Ah, I say too simple Helen, no too rustic,

do you think beauty can be without sin?

you must, either change your beauty or not be rough;

great beauty is strife with chastity.

114 Jupiter delights in this, golden Venus delights with theft;

this theft no doubt gave Jupiter as your father.

115 If forces in the seed of love could hardly be,

and you the daughter of Jupiter and Leda can be pure

116 Then still you are pure, while my troy will keep you,

and I beg that I be your only crime.

117 Now we shall sin what the hour of our marriage will set right

if only Venus did not promise void to me.

118 But your husband persuades you to this thing, without voice,

and to not hinder the intrigue of his guest, he is away.

119 He has time no more suitable, to see his Cretan Kingdom –

Oh a wonderfully cunning man!

'the affair, of the man of Ida I enjoin to you,' he said leaving,

'you shall take care of our gust, my wife.'

you neglect your husband's order in his absence, I am a witness;

your utmost care is not to your guest.

120 Do you hope that this mindless man, my Tyndaris,

can sufficiently understand the gift of your beauty?

you are wrong: he is ignorant, if he thought you to be a great thing,

which he holds, he would not trust you to a stranger.

121 Even if you are not roused by my voice and ardour,

I am forced to enjoy this advantage:

or I am foolish, even surpassing himself,

if I allow a time so safe to go by idle.

122 Your lover was almost led to you hand;

use your husband's order with innocence!

you lie alone through nights so long in your empty bed;

I too lie alone on my empty bed.

123 te mihi meque tibi communia gaudia iungant;
    candidior medio nox erit illa die.
124 tunc ego iurabo quaevis tibi numina meque
    adstringam verbis in sacra vestra meis;
tunc ego, si non est fallax fiducia nostri,
    efficiam praesens, ut mea regna petas.
125 si pudet et metuis ne me videare secuta,
    ipse reus sine te criminis huius ero.
126 nam sequar Aegidae factum fratrumque tuorum;
    exemplo tangi non propiore potes.
127 te rapuit Theseus, geminas Leucippidas illi;
    quartus in exemplis adnumerabor ego.
128 Troia classis adest armis instructa virisque;
    iam facient celeres remus et aura vias.
129 ibis Dardanias ingens regina per urbes,
    teque novam credet vulgus adesse deam,
quaque feres gressus, adolebunt cinnama flammae,
    caesaque sanguineam victima planget humum.
130 dona pater fratresque et cum genetrice sorores
    Iliadesque omnes totaque Troia dabit.
131 ei mihi! pars a me vix dicitur ulla futuri.
    132 plura feres quam quae littera nostra refert.
133 nec tu rapta time, ne nos fera bella sequantur,
    concitet et vires Graecia magna suas.
134 tot prius abductis ecqua est repetita per arma?
    crede mihi, vanos res habet ista metus.
135 nomine ceperunt Aquilonis Erechthida Thraces
    et tuta a bello Bistonis ora fuit.
136 Phasida puppe nova vexit Pagasaeus Iason,
    laesa neque est Colcha Thessala terra manu.
137 te quoque qui rapuit, rapuit Minoida Theseus;
    nulla tamen Minos Cretas ad arma vocat.
138 terror in his ipso maior solet esse periclo;
    quaeque timere libet, pertimuisse pudet.
139 finge tamen, si vis, ingens consurgere bellum:
    et mihi sunt vires, et mea tela nocent.
140 nec minor est Asiae quam vestrae copia terrae:
    illa viris dives, dives abundat equis.
141 nec plus Atrides animi Menelaus habebit
    quam Paris aut armis anteferendus erit.
142 paene puer caesis abducta armenta recepi
    hostibus et causam nominis inde tuli.
143 paene puer iuvenes vario certamine vici,
    in quibus Ilioneus Deiphobusque fuit.
144 neve putes, non me nisi comminus esse timendum,
    figitur in iusso nostra sagitta loco.

123 You to me and me to you join in mutual delights;
the middle of the night will be brighter than day.
124 Then I will swear to whatever gods you choose and
I will be obliged to you by my words to you rites;
then I, if my confidence is not deceptive,
I will immediately complete, your desire to my kingdom.
125 If you are ashamed and afraid that you are seen to follow me,
I will be guilty of this crime with you.
126 For I will follow the deed of Aegeus's son and of your brothers;
you can be touched by no closer example.
127 Theseus abducted you, the twins took the daughters of Leucippus.
I will be counted as the fourth example.
128 The fleet of troy is here equipped with men and arms;
soon wind and oar will send us swift on our journey.
129 A great queen you will go through the Dardanian cities,
and the public will think you are the new goddess here,
every step you take, will burn a cinnamon flame,
and slain victims will plunge to the blood-stained ground.
130 My father, brothers, mother, sisters
and all of Illiam and the whole of Troy will bring you gifts.
131 Ah to me! I can barely speak of any part of what will happen.
132 More you will receive than more letters mention.
133 Don't fear if you are taken, beastly war will follow us,
and mighty Greece summons her might.
134 Of the so many abducted before has any been returned by an army?
Believe me, that matter is fear in vain.
135 In the name of Aquilo the Thracians captured Erechtheus' daughter
and the Bistonian shores were safe from war.
136 Jason of Pagasa in his new ship carried away the Phasian girl,
and the land of Thessaly was not harmed by the Colchian hand.
137 Likewise Thesesu who took you, took the Minotaur;
in spite of this Minos did not call for Cretans to take up arms.
138 The fear in these matters is often greater than the danger itself;
it causes pleasure for all to fear, it causes all shame to fear greatly.
139 However pretend, if you wish, that a mighty war is risen:
and I have my men and my weapons can do harm.
140 Neither is Asia less wealthy than your country:
she overflows with wealth of men and horses.
141 Neither does Menelaus of Atreus have more spirit
than Paris nor is he superior in arms.
142 When only a boy I took back my stolen herds slaying the enemy
and thenceforth I bore the name.
143 When only a boy I conquered young men in various contests
in which were Ilion and Deiphobus.
144 And don't you think, that I am only feared in close combat
I can pierce with my arrow anywhere you wish.

145 num potes haec illi primae dare facta iuventae,
 instruere Atriden num potes arte mea?
omnia si dederis, numquid dabis Hectora fratrem?
 unus is innumeri militis instar erit.
146 quid valeam nescis et te mea robora fallunt;
 ignoras cui sis nupta futura viro.
147 aut igitur nullo belli repetere tumultu,
 aut cedent Marti Dorica castra meo.
148 nec tamen indigner pro tanta sumere ferrum
 coniuge; certamen praemia magna movent.
149 tu quoque, si de te totus contenderit orbis,
 nomen ab aeterna posteritate feres
spe modo non timida dis hinc egressa secundis
 exige cum plena munera pacta fide.

145 Are you able to show me deeds like these in his early youth,
can you train the son of Atreus in my art?
if you give all this, can you give him Hector as a brother?
he alone will be worth countless soldiers.
146 You don't know my strength and my strength deceives you;
you don't know the man whom you will be his future bride.
147 And so either they demand your return without the uproar of war,
or the Doric camp will fall to me in war.
148 However neither will I be indignant to take up arms for such a
wife; great prizes creates competition.
149 You too, if the whole world contends for you,
you will bear an eternal name to all prosperity
only take hope, send away your fears, the gods' fortune we have
claim with my full service pledged in faith.

HELEN TO PARIS
OVID'S HEROIDES XVII

1 Si mihi quae legi, Pari, non legisse liceret,
    servarem numeros sicut et ante probae.
2 Nunc oculos tua cum violarit epistula nostros,
    non rescribendi gloria visa levis.
3 ausus es hospitii temeratis advena sacris
    legitimam nuptae sollicitare fidem!
scilicet idcirco ventosa per aequora vectum
    excepit portu Taenaris ora suo
nec tibi, diversa quamvis e gente venires,
    oppositas habuit regia nostra fores,
esset ut officii merces iniuria tanti?
    qui sic intrabas, hospes an hostis eras?
nec dubito quin haec, cum sit tam iusta, vocetur
    rustica iudicio nostra querela tuo.
4 rustica sim sane, dum non oblita pudoris
    dumque tenor vitae sit sine labe meae.
5 si non est ficto tristis mihi vultus in ore
    nec sedeo duris torva superciliis,
fama tamen clara est, et adhuc sine crimine lusi
    et laudem de me nullus adulter habet.
6 quo magis admiror, quae sit fiducia coepti
    spemque tori dederit quae tibi causa mei.
7 an quia vim nobis Neptunius attulit heros,
    rapta semel videor bis quoque digna rapi?
crimen erat nostrum, si delenita fuissem;
    cum sim rapta, meum quid nisi nolle fuit?
non tamen e facto fructum tulit ille petitum;
    excepto redii passa timore nihil.
8 oscula luctanti tantummodo pauca protervus
    abstulit: ulterius nil habet ille mei.
9 quae tua nequitia est, non his contenta fuisset.
10   di melius! similis non fuit ille tui.
11 reddidit intactam minuitque modestia crimen
    et iuvenem facti paenituisse patet.
12 Thesea paenituit, Paris ut succederet illi,
    ne quando nomen non sit in ore meum?
nec tamen irascor—quis enim succenset amanti?—
    si modo, quem praefers, non simulatur amor.
13 hoc quoque enim dubito, non quod fiducia desit,
    aut mea sit facies non bene nota mihi,
sed quia credulitas damno solet esse puellis
    verbaque dicuntur vestra carere fide.

1 If I might have not read what I read, Paris,
I might save my good regards for you just like before.
2 Now my eyes have been violated by your letter
I have honor in not replying lightly.
3 You are a stranger who dared to violate the sacred oath of hospitality
to tempt the lawful loyalty of a wife!
of course carried through windy seas
the Taenarian shores accepted you into its asylum,
although you come from a different kind of people,
my kingdom did not have closed gates to you,
it is an insult for a reward for such a service?
you who enters, are you friend or foe?
No doubt in this, with it so justified, my complaint
is called rustic in your judgment.
4 Certainly let me be rustic, then I am not daubed with shame
and then the course of my life is without fall.
5 If there is not a constant sad countenance on my face
or if I don't sit with a grim harsh brow,
my reputation is yet clear, and I have entertained myself without sin
and no adulterer has my praise.
6 I wonder what more, which your confidence has begun
and it is the reason you give tome to hope for my bed.
7 Because the Neptunian hero bore force with me,
having been taken once am I seen to be fit to taken again?
the crime was mine, if I had been seduced;
having been taken like I was, what could I do except refuse?
however he did not bare the fruit he sought from his deeds;
I returned home unharmed except by fright.
8 The shameless man merely took a few fighting kisses:
he had nothing more from me.
9 which your depravity, might have not been content with.
10 Gods do better for me! he was not like you.
11 He returned me untouched and his modesty diminished his crime
and it is clear the young man regretted what he did.
12 Theseus repented, so that Paris could succeed him,
when will my name cease in the mouths of men?
however I am not angry – for who is inflamed with angry by a lover –
if only the love which you offer is not simulated.
13 For I doubt this also, not because assurance is lacking,
or my beauty is not well known to me,
but because credulity is usually damaging to girls
and they say your words are without truth.

14 at peccant aliae, matronaque rara pudica est.
15   quis prohibet raris nomen inesse meum?
nam mea quod visa est tibi mater idonea, cuius
    exemplo flecti me quoque posse putes,
matris in admisso falsa sub imagine lusae
    error inest; pluma tectus adulter erat.
16 nil ego, si peccem, possum nescisse; nec ullus
    error qui facti crimen obumbret erit.
17 illa bene erravit vitiumque auctore redemit.
18   felix in culpa quo Iove dicar ego?
et genus et proavos et regia nomina iactas;
    clara satis domus haec nobilitate sua est.
19 Iuppiter ut soceri proavus taceatur et omne
    Tantalidae Pelopis Tyndareique decus;
dat mihi Leda Iovem cygno decepta parentem,
    quae falsam gremio credula fovit avem.
20 i nunc et Phrygiae late primordia gentis
    cumque suo Priamum Laumedonte refer!
quos ego suspicio; sed qui tibi gloria magna est
    quintus, is a nostro nomine primus erit.
21 sceptra tuae quamvis rear esse potentia terrae,
    non tamen haec illis esse minora puto.
22 si iam divitiis locus hic numeroque virorum
    vincitur, at certe barbara terra tua est.
23 munera tanta quidem promittit epistula dives
    ut possint ipsas illa movere deas.
24 sed si iam vellem fines transire pudoris,
    tu melior culpae causa futurus eras.
25 aut ego perpetuo famam sine labe tenebo
    aut ego te potius quam tua dona sequar.
26 utque ea non sperno, sic acceptissima semper
    munera sunt, auctor quae pretiosa facit.
27 plus multo est, quod amas, quod sum tibi causa laboris,
    quod per tam longas spes tua venit aquas.
28 illa quoque, adposita quae nunc facis, improbe, mensa,
    quamvis experiar dissimulare, noto—
cum modo me spectas oculis, lascive, protervis,
    quos vix instantes lumina nostra ferunt,
et modo suspiras, modo pocula proxima nobis
    sumis, quaque bibi, tu quoque parte bibis.
29 a, quotiens digitis, quotiens ego tecta notavi
    signa supercilio paene loquente dari!
et saepe extimui ne vir meus illa videret,
    non satis occultis erubuique notis.
30 saepe vel exiguo vel nullo murmure dixi:
    'nil pudet hunc!' nec vox haec mea falsa fuit.

14 But others sin, and a chaste wife is rare.

15 Who keeps my name in the rare?
for because my mother seems fit for you, by whose
example you think to are also able to prevail upon me too,
you are mistaken because she fell into adultery under a false illusion;
the adulterer was concealed by feathers.

16 If I sin I cannot be ignorant;
nor any error which could cloud the deeds of my crime.

17 She errored was well and her crime redeemed by god.

18 With what Jove should I be called lucky in my crime?
but you utter your people and ancestors and royal name;
this house is famous enough with its own nobility.

19 Not to speak of Jupiter my husband's ancestor
and all the honor of Pelops son of Tantalus and of Tyndareus;
Leda having been deceived by a swan gave me Jove as a parent,
who trustingly nurtured the illusion of the bird in her lap.

20 Go now and tell me the extensive origins of the Phrygian race
and of Paris and his father Laomedon!
I respect them; but he who is your greatest glory is fifth from you,
Jupiter is first from my name.

21 although I imagine the scepter to be power in your land
however don't think the ones of ours are less mighty.

22 If this place is indeed greater in wealth and number of men,
then certainly your country is a barbaric.

23 Indeed you letter promises such rich gifts
that it is able to move the gods themselves.

24 But if I now wished to cross the borders of chastity,
you would be the better cause of my crime.

25 Either I constantly hold my reputation without fault
or I follow you rather than your gifts.

26 Even I don't reject them, gifts are always most acceptable,
when the giver makes them precious.

27 It is more that you love me, so I am the cause of your labors,
because your hope comes over such far waters.

28 Also, I notice what you do when the tables are laid,
shameless man, indeed I try hide –
when you only stare at my with your eyes, lustful, audacious,
whose insistent gaze my eyes can hardly bare,
and now you sigh, and soon you take the cup nearest to me,
and where I drank from, you drink from the same place.

29 Ah, how many times I noticed your fingers,
you concealed signs given from your almost speaking eyebrows!
and often I am afraid that my husband sees them,
and I redden at the signs you don't hide enough.

30 Often even inadequate murmurs or nothing at all I said:
'this man is shameless!' Neither has this voice been false.

31 orbe quoque in mensae legi sub nomine nostro,
  quod deducta mero littera fecit, 'amo.'
32 credere me tamen hoc oculo renuente negavi.
33   ei mihi, iam didici sic ego posse loqui!
his ego blanditiis, si peccatura fuissem,
  flecterer; his poterant pectora nostra capi.
34 est quoque, confiteor, facies tibi rara potestque
  velle sub amplexus ire puella tuos.
35 altera sed potius felix sine crimine fiat,
  quam cadat externo noster amore pudor.
36 disce modo exemplo formosis posse carere;
  est virtus placitis abstinuisse bonis.
37 quam multos credis iuvenes optare, quod optas?
  qui sapiant, oculos an Paris unus habes?
non tu plus cernis, sed plus temerarius audes;
  nec tibi plus cordis sed minus oris, adest.
38 tunc ego te vellem celeri venisse carina,
  cum mea virginitas mille petita procis.
39 si te vidissem, primus de mille fuisses;
  iudicio veniam vir dabit ipse meo.
40 ad possessa venis praeceptaque gaudia serus;
  spes tua lenta fuit; quod petis, alter habet.
41 ut tamen optarim fieri tua Troica coniunx,
  invitam sic me nec Menelaus habet.
42 desine molle, precor, verbis convellere pectus
  neve mihi, quam te dicis amare, noce;
sed sine quam tribuit sortem fortuna tueri
  nec spolium nostri turpe pudoris habe.
43 at Venus hoc pacta est, et in altae vallibus Idae
  tres tibi se nudas exhibuere deae;
unaque cum regnum, belli daret altera laudem
  'Tyndaridis coniunx,' tertia dixit, 'eris!'
credere vix equidem caelestia corpora possum
  arbitrio formam supposuisse tuo;
utque sit hoc verum, certe pars altera ficta est,
  iudicii pretium qua data dicor ego.
44 non est tanta mihi fiducia corporis, ut me
  maxima teste dea dona fuisse putem.
45 contenta est oculis hominum mea forma probari;
  laudatrix Venus est invidiosa mihi.
46 sed nihil infirmo; faveo quoque laudibus istis;
  nam, mens, vox quare, quod cupit esse, neget?
nec tu succense nimium mihi creditus aegre;
  tarda solet magnis rebus inesse fides.
47 prima mea est igitur Veneri placuisse voluptas;
  proxima, me visam praemia summa tibi,

31 Also I read in on the round table beneath my name,
which letters having been laid out by wine, 'I love.'
32 Yet I refuse to believe this with my eyes I refuse.
33 Ah me, now I learnt how to speak like so!
these are the flattery, if I had sinned,
that might distract me; these could have captured my heart.
34 Also I confess you are a rare beauty
and a girl could want to go into your arms.
35 But others could be made happier without sin,
rather than my reputation falling to a foreign lover.
36 Learn by example on how to live deprived of beauty;
virtue is abstaining from pleasuring delights.
37 How many youths do you believe long for what you desire?
are they wise, or is Paris the one who has eyes?
you see no more, but you are more reckless;
neither are you wiser but less composed.
38 Then I wish your swift ship has come,
when a thousand suitors seek my virginity.
39 If I had seen you, you would be first of the thousand;
my man himself will come and give pardon to my judgement.
40 You come too late to joys possessed and commanded;
you hope was slow; what you seek, another possesses.
41 Yet although I chose to be made your bride in Troy,
Menelaus does not have me here against my will.
42 Stop shattering my heart with soft words, I beg,
whom you say you love, don't hurt me;
but to maintain the fortune fate has bestowed
and don't scandalously create a spoil of my chastity.
43 But Venus promised this, and in the deep valleys of Ida
three naked goddesses revealed themselves to you;
and while one offered you a kingdom, the other offering fame in war
'Helen will be your wife!' the third said,
as for me I am able to scarcely believe that celestial bodies
were place under your judgement for their beauty;
and if this is true, surely the other parts are feigned,
that I was said to be offered as a payment for your judgement.
44 I don't have so much trust in my body, that I
am the greatest gift the goddess could think of.
45 I am content that the eyes of men commend my beauty;
the praise of Venus is invidious.
46 But I dispute nothing; I also favor your praises
because, my soul, why deny the voice which is to be desire?
don't be inflamed with anger if your trust to me too comes painfully
it is usual for loyalty in great things to come slowly.
47 Therefore my greatest pleasure is to have please Venus;
next, you saw me as the upmost prize,

nec te Palladios nec te Iunonis honores
    auditis Helenae praeposuisse bonis.
48 ergo ego sum virtus, ego sum tibi nobile regnum?
    ferrea sim, si non hoc ego pectus amem.
49 ferrea, crede mihi, non sum; sed amare repugno
    illum, quem fieri vix puto posse meum.
50 quid bibulum curvo proscindere litus aratro
    spemque sequi coner quam locus ipse negat?
sum rudis ad Veneris furtum nullaque fidelem —
    di mihi sunt testes!—lusimus arte virum!
nunc quoque, quod tacito mando mea verba libello,
    fungitur officio littera nostra novo.
51 felices, quibus usus adest! ego nescia rerum
    difficilem culpae suspicor esse viam.
52 ipse malo metus est; iam nunc confundor et omnes
    in nostris oculos vultibus esse reor.
53 nec reor hoc falso; sensi mala murmura vulgi
    et quasdam voces rettulit Aethra mihi.
54 at tu dissimula, nisi si desistere mavis.
55   sed cur desistas? dissimulare potes.
56 lude, sed occulte! maior, non maxima, nobis
    est data libertas, quod Menelaus abest.
57 ille quidem procul est, ita re cogente, profectus;
    magna fuit subitae iustaque causa viae;
aut mihi sic visum est; ego, cum dubitaret an iret,
    'quam primum,' dixi, 'fac rediturus eas!'
omine laetatus dedit oscula, 'resque domusque
    et tibi sit curae Troicus hospes,' ait.
58 vix tenui risum, quem dum conpescere luctor,
    nil illi potui dicere praeter 'erit.'
59 uela quidem Creten ventis dedit ille secundis;
    sed tu non ideo cuncta licere puta!
sic meus hinc vir abest ut me custodiat absens.
60   an nescis longas regibus esse manus?
forma quoque est oneri; nam quo constantius ore
    laudamur vestro, iustius ille timet.
61 quae iuvat, ut nunc est, eadem mihi gloria damno est,
    et melius famae verba dedisse fuit.
62 nec quod abest hic me tecum mirare relictam;
    moribus et vitae credidit ille meae.
63 de facie metuit, vitae confidit, et illum
    securum probitas, forma timere facit.
64 tempora ne pereant ultro data praecipis, utque
    simplicis utamur commoditate viri.
65 et libet et timeo, nec adhuc exacta voluntas
    est satis; in dubio pectora nostra labant.

and you preferred neither the honor of Athena nor Juno
to the beauty of Helen that you have heard.
48 Therefore I am virtue, I am a noble kingdom to you?
I am made out of iron, if I did not love this heart of yours.
49 Trust me, I am not iron; but I oppose to love
he, who I think hardly could become mine.
50 Why plough through wet shores with a curved blade
and try to follow the hope that this place denies?
I am unskilled in the theft of love and never true –
the gods be my witness! – have I deceived my husband with artifice!
likewise now, I confide my words to this silent letter,
my letter administers a new duty.
51 Happy, those who are experienced! I unaware of these affairs
suspect the path of sin to be difficult.
52 Fear itself is bad; now I am confused
and I reckon all eyes to be on my expressions.
53 I don't think this is false; I feel the belligerent murmurs of the public
and Aethra brings to me their remarks.
54 But conceal your love, unless you want to end it.
55 But why end it? You can hide.
56 Play, but secretly! I have been given more freedom,
but not all my liberty, because Menelaus is away.
57 He advances far away, compelled by matters;
there was a great and justified cause for his sudden journey;
or ass it seemed to me; I, when he hesitated about going,
said, 'Go and make your return at first!'
happy at the omen he gave me kisses, 'the affairs and house
and the worry the Trojan guest are yours' he said.
58 I could hardly hold my laughter, which I restrained with a struggle,
with that I could say nothing expect for 'It will be.'
59 He gave sail for Crete with a second wind;
but don't think for that reason all is allowed!
Although my husband is absent like this being away he guards me.
60 Or do you not know that a king's power reaches far?
also beauty is a burden; for I am praised constantly
by the mouths of your people, he is justified to be more afraid.
61 That glory which delights me, as it is now, dooms me,
it would be better to give away the words of fame.
62 Don't be amazed that he is absent leaving me here with you;
he trusts my principles and my way of life.
63 He fears my beauty, he trusts my way of life,
and my honesty makes him carefree, and to be afraid of beauty.
64 You teach that a later given time is time that is lost,
and so I will make use of the convenience of a simple minded husband.
65 I desire and I fear, neither has my lust yet concluded;
my heart wavers in doubt.

66 et vir abest nobis et tu sine coniuge dormis,
  inque vicem tua me, te mea forma capit;
et longae noctes et iam sermone coimus
  et tu, me miseram! blandus, et una domus.
67 et peream, si non invitant omnia culpam;
  nescio quo tardor sed tamen ipsa metu.
68 quod male persuades, utinam bene cogere posses!
  vi mea rusticitas excutienda fuit.
69 utilis interdum est ipsis iniuria passis.
70   sic certe felix esse coacta forem.
71 dum novus est, potius coepto pugnemus amori!
  flamma recens parva sparsa resedit aqua.
72 certus in hospitibus non est amor; errat, ut ipsi,
  cumque nihil speres firmius esse, fugit.
73 Hypsipyle testis, testis Minoia virgo est;
  in non exhibitis utraque lusa toris.
74 tu quoque dilectam multos, infide, per annos
  diceris Oenonen destituisse tuam.
75 nec tamen ipse negas; et nobis omnia de te
  quaerere, si nescis, maxima cura fuit.
76 adde quod, ut cupias constans in amore manere,
  non potes; expediunt iam tua vela Phryges;
dum loqueris mecum, dum nox sperata paratur,
  qui ferat in patriam, iam tibi ventus erit.
77 cursibus in mediis novitatis plena relinques
  gaudia; cum ventis noster abibit amor.
78 an sequar, ut suades, laudataque Pergama visam
  pronurus et magni Laumedontis ero?
non ita contemno volucris praeconia famae,
  ut probris terras impleat illa meis.
79 quid de me poterit Sparte, quid Achaia tota,
  quid gentes Asiae, quid tua Troia loqui?
quid Priamus de me, Priami quid sentiet uxor
  totque tui fratres Dardanidesque nurus?
tu quoque qui poteris fore me sperare fidelem
  et non exemplis anxius esse tuis?
quicumque Iliacos intraverit advena portus,
  is tibi solliciti causa timoris erit.
80 ipse mihi quotiens iratus 'adultera!' dices,
  oblitus nostro crimen inesse tuum!
delicti fies idem reprehensor et auctor.
81   terra, precor, vultus obruat ante meos!
at fruar Iliacis opibus cultuque beato
  donaque promissis uberiora feram:
purpura nempe mihi pretiosaque texta dabuntur,
  congestoque auri pondere dives ero!

66 And my husband is absent and you sleep without a wife,
my beauty captures you, and yours conquers me;
and the nights are long and we meet for conversations
and you, oh me! seductive, and one house.
67 And let me die, if all does not invite my crime;
I don't know why I am hesitant but because of fear itself.
68 If only you could rightly force, that which you wrongly persuade!
my idiocy would leave me with force.
69 Sometimes wrongdoing is useful for those who suffer it.
70 At least then I might be forced to be happy.
71 While it is new, w should fight more the beginning of love!
a new flame is extinguished with a small sprinkle of water.
72 Love is not fixed in a guest; it wanders, like himself,
and when you expect nothing to be more powerful, it vanishes.
73 Hypsipyle is a witness, and so is the Minoan virgin;
both played in concealed beds.
74 You also left Oenone as they say, unfaithful man,
whom you loved for many years.
75 However you don't denied it; to search all bout you,
if you did not know, was my greatest care.
76 Add to which, that even if you wish to remain unchanging in love,
you couldn't; your Phrygians are already preparing the sails;
while you speak with me, while you prepare for a longed for night,
there soon will be a wind, which carries you back to your fatherland.
77 You relinquish complete delights in the midway through its novelty;
our love will depart with the wind.
78 Or should I follow, as you say, and see the Pergamon you praise
and be the granddaughter in law of the great Laomedon?
though I would not disregard the wings of spreading rumors,
if the land were filled with my disgrace.
79 What would Sparta, what would all of Achaia,
what would people of Asian, what would your Troy say?
what would Priam and his wife
and all your brothers and Trojan daughters in law feel about me?
How could you also hope for me to be loyal
and not be anxious at your example of yourself?
All strangers entering the ports of Ilion,
would be a cause of restless fear to you.
80 How often you being angry with me would say, 'adulteress!'
forgetting my crime belongs to you!
you become the blamer and author of my crime.
81 I pray, before this the earth buries my face!
but I will enjoy Ilion's wealth and prosperous culture
and I'll bare gifts more fruitful than you promised:
no doubt purple and precious fabrics will be given to me,
and I will be wealthy having collected piles of gold!

da veniam fassae! non sunt tua munera tanti;
    nescio quo tellus me tenet ista modo.
82 quis mihi, si laedar, Phrygiis succurret in oris?
    unde petam fratres, unde parentis opem?
omnia Medeae fallax promisit Iason:
    pulsa est Aesonia num minus illa domo?
non erat Aeetes, ad quem despecta rediret,
    non Idyia parens Chalciopeve soror.
83 tale nihil timeo, sed nec Medea timebat;
    fallitur augurio spes bona saepe suo.
84 omnibus invenies, quae nunc iactantur in alto,
    navibus a portu lene fuisse fretum.
85 fax quoque me terret, quam se peperisse cruentam
    ante diem partus est tua visa parens;
et vatum timeo monitus, quos igne Pelasgo
    Ilion arsurum praemonuisse ferunt.
86 utque favet Cytherea tibi, quia vicit habetque
    parta per arbitrium bina tropaea tuum,
sic illas vereor, quae, si tua gloria vera est,
    iudice te causam non tenuere duae;
nec dubito, quin te si prosequar arma parentur.
87   ibit per gladios, ei mihi! noster amor.
88 an fera Centauris indicere bella coegit
    Atracis Haemonios Hippodamia viros:
tu fore tam iusta lentum Menelaon in ira
    et geminos fratres Tyndareumque putas?
quod bene te iactes et fortia facta loquaris,
    a verbis facies dissidet ista suis.
89 apta magis Veneri quam sunt tua corpora Marti.
90   bella gerant fortes, tu, Pari, semper ama!
Hectora, quem laudas, pro te pugnare iubeto;
    militia est operis altera digna tuis.
91 his ego, si saperem pauloque audacior essem,
    uterer; utetur, siqua puella sapit.
92 aut ego deposito sapiam fortasse pudore
    et dabo cunctatas tempore victa manus.
93 quod petis, ut furtim praesentes ista loquamur,
    scimus, quid captes conloquiumque voces;
sed nimium properas, et adhuc tua messis in herba est.
94   haec mora sit voto forsan amica tuo.
95 hactenus; arcanum furtivae conscia mentis
    littera iam lasso pollice sistat opus.
96 cetera per socias Clymenen Aethramque loquamur,
    quae mihi sunt comites consiliumque duae.

Forgive me for saying it! Your gifts are not worth so much;
I don't know this land which would merely hold me.
82 If I am hurt, who will run to help me in the Phrygian shores?
from where will I seek for brothers, from where the help of parents?
deceitful Jason promised Medea everything:
no less was not she expelled from the house of Aeson?
There was no Aeetes, to whom she disdained could return to,
no parent Idyia no sister Chalciope.
83 I fear nothing like such, but nor did Medea fear;
hope is often deceived by its own augury of good.
84 You will find every ship, which is now thrown in the deep,
the seas gentle for them in the harbor.
85 The torch also frightens me, which born to her blood-stained
was seen by your mother before the day of your birth;
and I fear the prophet's warning, who foretold
that Ilion would be burn with a Pelasgian fire.
86 And as much as Venus favors you, because she won and holds
a double trophy secured from your judgement,
then I am afraid of the others, which, if your glory were true,
no longer hold their cause because of your judgement;
no doubt, If I followed you then war would be prepared.
87 Alas! Our love will travel through sword.
88 Or Hippodamia of Atrax forced the Haemonia's men
to declare fierce war on the Centaurs:
do you think Menelaus will be slow to righteous anger
and will the Twins, his brothers, or Tyndareus?
for you good boasts and talks of courageous deeds,
you beauty disagrees with your words.
89 Your body is more suited for Venus than for Mars.
90 The brave wage war, you, Paris, always love!
order Hector, whom you praise, to fight for you;
you skills are worthy in another battle.
91 If I were to taste them and be a little more bold,
I could enjoy them, if any girl tastes it, she could.
92 Or perhaps putting down my chastity I could taste it
and hesitancy conquered by time I will give you my hand.
93 I know what you seek, tell me secretly when we are together,
what you hope to capture in our conversations;
but you are too hasty, and thus grass are your harvest.
94 This delay perhaps will be a liking to your pledge.
95 As far as this; now the labor letter of the mysteries
of my secret heart cease with my tiring fingers .
96 I will tell the rest through my friends Clymene and Aethra,
who are my two companions and my counsels.

Printed in Great Britain
by Amazon

36384410R00040